'TIS THE SEASON

'TIS THE SEASON

WELCOME TO LILY ROCK HOLIDAY MYSTERY
BOOK 1

BONNIE HARDY

'TIS THE SEASON

WELCOME TO LILY ROCK HOLIDAY MYSTERY
BOOK 1

BONNIE HARDY

Copyright © 2022 Bonnie Hardy

eBook ISBN: 978-1-954995-10-9

Paperback ISBN: 978-1-954995-11-6

Cover Design by Ebook Launch

Editing by Proof Positive

GET A FREE SHORT STORY

Join my VIP newsletter to get the latest news of Lily Rock along with contests, discounts, events, and giveaways! I'll also send you *Meadow's Hat*, a short story set before book one :).

Sign up on bonniehardywrites.com/newsletter

A STRIPPER OR A MY LITTLE PONY?

"So you want me to go undercover in Lily Rock?" She burst out laughing. "And to call myself Dixie Jones?" She could hardly keep the incredulity from her voice. "Why do I have to go undercover? It's a small town. I can make this a one and done using my own name."

The captain cleared his throat. "The police academy made an exception for you from day one. We took into consideration your years of experience in McClure, Ohio. Since Los Angeles can be a culture shock, you agreed to go through our police academy for a year; we're starting you out with soft undercover work in a small town like you're used to. And as for your name, anyone could look you up and find out you're a police officer, so Dixie Jones is your new identity and that's that. You don't have a choice."

She wanted to resist. Push back on his boring review of her decision to return to school. But she bit her tongue instead. "Yes, sir," came out of her mouth, almost as if she really meant it.

"And you've done a good job," he continued. "You've passed every test well ahead of the other recruits. That's why your name was first on the academy's mind when this Lily Rock thing came up. And if you do this well? We'll make sure you get the top pick of assignments after graduation. How's that for incentive?"

I know there's a catch. There always is. But I can't refuse. It would be rude, considering how the captain stood up for me since the beginning. "Can you tell me more about the Lily Rock situation?"

"The unofficial town council—they call themselves the Old Rockers—are worried about an increase in theft and crimes this past year. And then something about bad Yelp reviews on the internet. At least that's what the anonymous emails say. From what I can tell, the town is growing and the usual ways of keeping people in line aren't working as well."

She kept her comments to herself, waiting for the captain to continue.

"I want you to go undercover right before Christmas. You can use your experience to get to know people and find out who's writing the anonymous emails and more about the crime situation."

She repressed a deep sigh. "So can you tell me more about the undercover part?"

"Gather the information to determine, in your professional opinion, just what Lily Rock needs. Write a detailed report and get it to me by Christmas."

She held the cell phone away from her ear to think. *I really want a job that's higher profile. More bad guys and lots of chases. Otherwise, I'd have stayed in McClure.*

She brought the cell back to her ear. "Are you sure I'm right for the job?"

"Don't question my decision," he barked.

Geez, I just asked. Don't get your tail in a knot. "Sorry, sir. Can you tell me more about the emails?"

A blustery sigh filled her ear. "We tracked the IP address to the local library. There are three emails. I can send you all of the information." His voice grew louder. "About the other thing, the bad reviews? I can't control social media. I have enough trouble on the streets."

Settle down, Captain. I hear you. Not like I have other plans for the holidays. I used to work in small towns just like Lily Rock, but I never expected you'd remember, let alone make me actually go undercover there.

"I'm ready for the assignment." *Check it out. I really sound cooperative. Little does he know...*

"That's the spirit," he said with a fake chuckle. Then he hung up.

The scent of coffee, rich and aromatic, wafted from the kitchen. As enticing as it smelled, she hesitated, taking time to consider her next step. *He wants me undercover; I'll pretend I'm a tourist. That works in my favor. I won't make any personal connections. No one will know my real name. In and out, bada boom bada bing. Then back to the academy. Maybe this is a good thing. I'll forget my misgivings and actually do some work.*

When she'd decided to rejoin the police academy, she'd thought she had everything planned. She made a move to get out of her small town, but she told them she'd take a similar assignment, so long as she was in Los Angeles.

The oldest in her class, she thought she knew what she wanted. But the closer she came to graduating, the less certain she became. She had a mentor and the captain was very supportive. But the new city and job didn't feel quite right. Not even after a year.

She turned slightly, catching sight of the mirror on the wall. Staring at her reflection, she spoke aloud. "Hello, Dixie Jones." *Can that name get any more small town?* She picked up her phone and called the captain on redial. The other end clicked. Before he could talk she began.

"With a name like Dixie I'm either a stripper or a My Little Pony. I can be a tourist, but what's the rest of my backstory, if you don't mind me asking?"

She put him on speaker. "Uh-huh," she said as she walked to the kitchen. She lay the cell on the counter to pour herself a large mug of coffee. Bending over, she muttered into the speaker, "Uh-huh," for the second time.

I sure wound him up. Made my morning, listening to his bluster. Might as well start calling myself Dixie Jones. Otherwise I'll be found out before I can make any headway. Once in Lily Rock I'll be a pest and get all the dirt. Maybe they have real problems, but like what, I wonder? Trash in the park... A bad hair day on a Friday...dog poop left on the sidewalk?

She picked up the phone as the captain continued to yell. "Yes, sir." He ended the conversation quickly after that.

I missed pretty much everything he said. Oh well, I'll make up my own backstory. Probably won't be necessary. I don't plan on having any personal interactions. Gotta pack. Jeans, jacket, and some shirts. Boots. It may snow. I guess that's what they wear in Lily Rock.

Sitting on the sofa, she took her last sip of lukewarm coffee. *On the one hand, I could use a change of scenery. But on the other hand, I'll be all by myself in a strange place.*

She finished the last drop. *Okay then, let's get this over with.*

NO ROOM AT THE INN

"Drat, there's no place to park!" Dixie Jones pulled her truck to the side of the street to look around. She glanced at her phone for the address of the rental place called Lily Rock Realty. She looked up. Two trucks and a motorcycle parked in front of a small building. Posters advertising cabin rentals covered the outside, along with red, white, and blue streamers.

A large sign with the image of Smokey the Bear caught her eyes. He held a sign with both paws which read in bold letters: "Fire warning. Extreme." Dixie was not surprised. She knew all of the small towns in the San Gabriel forest were in the fire danger region, even this late in December before the first snow.

Every year a fire broke out. Sometimes arson, sometimes negligence, and often an electrical spark from an old wire. Volunteers remained at the ready to put out fires. Lately insurance companies refused to issue policies for homeowners. And when they did, the expense was so high most residents figured they'd go uninsured rather than pay the price.

Dixie glanced at her cell phone. Many of the cabins in Lily Rock were run by a central agency, where keys could be picked up and dropped off. She'd made a reservation the night before and then marked it on her list as her first expense. Once she made her deposit, Lily Rock Realty sent her a receipt and the directions. She'd pick up her key from them. *The department is gonna cover every last dime of this assignment.*

"Once more around the block," Jones muttered. She pulled away from the curb, and then slammed on her brakes. A small child running ahead of his mother crossed in the middle of the road. Sticking her head out the window, Dixie yelled, "Get your kid out of the street! Don't you realize my car weighs more than you and that kid put together?"

She wanted to cite the mother for endangering a minor. If she were a cop in Lily Rock, she might have done that. But fortunately she remembered she was undercover.

After two more trips around the block, Jones pulled into an empty parking space across from Lily Rock Realty. She'd been sent an email that her keys would be ready for pickup before noon. *Beep.* The truck locked. She looked both ways and then hurried across the road. A line had formed out the small doorway of the realtor's office. Standing at the end, she pulled out her phone to avoid making eye contact.

Out of the corner of her eye she saw a man wearing a felt bowler hat, moss-colored t-shirt, and slim black pants. He'd tied a red and black flannel shirt around his waist, and his hair had been pulled into a bun. The dark beard on his face contrasted with the gray color of his hair.

Jones smirked. *Looks like the hipsters have made it to Lily Rock. Must make the residents nuts.* She assumed anything new would make a small town like Lily Rock uncomfortable.

The man walked past her muttering, "They gave away my reservation. I'm so gonna Yelp them."

She hastily checked her own confirmation number. The

email said she had a reservation, but there was no official number or charge on her credit card. When it was her turn, she held the phone in front of the young kid's face. "I got a confirmation," she claimed.

He gave her a half smile. "That's not exactly what that email means. Here in Lily Rock, you don't count until you show up. I can't tell you how many people say they're coming and then only spend the day and drive back to LA without spending the night." He looked over her head toward the rest of the line and sniffed. "Smells like snow is coming," he mumbled.

"I didn't come here for a weather report," she retorted.

His eyes finally fixed on hers. "I'm afraid we gave your cabin to another customer. Or as they say, no room at this inn."

Jones shrugged. "Don't give me any of that seasonal nonsense. Do I look like a person who celebrates Christmas?" She waved the phone in front of his face again. *No wonder they're getting bad Yelp reviews. I guess the anonymous emailer had that right.*

She squinted to take a closer look at the name tag pinned to his shirt. "Okay, I see your name is Brad. So why don't you get me another room, Brad. Any cabin will do. Then I'll give you ten bucks to go spend at the arcade. Surely a place like this still has pinball."

Brad blinked. "Pinball?"

"Oh stop it. Don't play dumb with me. Give me the key."

He shook his head. "I can't take your ten bucks because the last cabin was rented an hour ago. I suggest you try down the street or get online. Airbnb may have a last-minute cancellation."

Jones noted his grimy hands, grease under his fingernails. "Do you normally work here?" she asked. *If I draw him into conversation maybe he'll find me a cabin. Personal connection, that's what they told me in class. Makes residents feel all warm and fuzzy.*

The kid stared at his hands. He held them up. "I work at my uncle's garage. I'm just stepping in here for the afternoon. If you live in Lily Rock, you take the jobs that come up. Gotta stay flexible."

Jets sighed. She knew for all practical purposes, it was senseless to try to wheedle a room from someone who really didn't have one. "Whatever happened to small-town hospitality?" she muttered. "Thanks for nothin'."

Across the street and back in the driver's seat, she placed both arms on the steering wheel. *This place is starting to get on my nerves.* After a brief search on the internet, she couldn't find anywhere else to stay one night, let alone two. She inhaled deeply, feeling her irritation get the better of her.

Taking another deep breath, she looked around. Lowering her window, she stuck her head outside and inhaled again, smiling. *The cold air feels great. Invigorating.* Even her lungs felt less congested when she took another deep breath. *I forgot the last time I actually inhaled without coughing.*

Shallow breathing in Los Angeles had become something she accepted about her new location. She'd learned to treat her shortness of breath like her unruly curly hair, something to tolerate and tuck away so as not to think about it too much.

Everyone at the academy smoked or vaped—outside, of course. But the secondhand smoke slipped inside through open doors. Exhaust from vehicles filled the entire city, smelling slightly acrid. After a while it got stuck in your nostrils.

She took another deep breath, exhaling slowly. *I kind of like this feeling. The people here are wacko but the air is pretty nice.*

Then her inner voice interrupted. *Stop it, Dixie. Don't go getting soft.*

Unsure about what to do next, she glanced down the boardwalk toward a lineup of small shops. Her thoughts drifted back to the academy, where she'd made an unexpected connection with a seasoned officer and instructor. Brian had led her through all of the difficult issues, including being older than the rest of the recruits.

"You have a mouth on you," he'd told her at their first meeting. Before she could retort he added, "But I like that. I like it a lot. In fact your mouth may be your greatest asset. Just be careful. The captain may not be a fan of you talking back."

She knew that comment had helped her just in time. She could have made a real problem for herself had she refused the Lily Rock assignment. She'd explain to the captain afterward about not wanting another small town. She'd tell him the fantastic academy training had broadened her horizons. *Everyone likes their ideas to be important.* After she wrote her Lily Rock report, he'd be more understanding. At least she hoped he would.

Her eyes rested on the library sign. *There you go. Small towns have helpful librarians. I'll step in and see what a local can do for my predicament.* She opened the truck door. *Plus I can look around to see if anyone is typing on a computer. Maybe catch the anonymous emailer in the act. Fast work, Dixie!*

She grinned and crossed the street again.

3

BORN TO BE WILD

In the middle of the road she heard the roar of a wide-open throttle. The sound grew louder. The thrumpy exhaust notes of a vintage classic motorcycle drew her glance. Others followed the first rider, a gang of motorcycles rumbled under the *Welcome to Lily Rock* sign. She hurried across the street to watch.

Within minutes the bikers filled the street. Riders wore black leather jackets and helmets that covered their heads and faces. Each rolled their bike under the *Welcome to Lily Rock* sign, making their presence known, gunning their engines as if to say, "We're here!"

Dragging her eyes from the gang, she looked at the crowd on the boardwalk. People watched with their mouths open. One woman pushed her child behind her, as if fearing for their safety.

She watched the lead rider as he maneuvered his ride into the dirt parking lot next to a place called Lola's. *Must be the local bar.* The rest of the bikes followed, pulling up next to each other. The lot overflowed with motorcycles and people in black leather. As the engine noise died down, riders popped off their bikes, and Dixie could see the backs of their jackets.

"Lola's" had been stitched in large white letters.

Okay, this might be trouble. Hard to tell from a distance. She knew the truth. At the academy, she'd learned that only one percent of motorcycle gangs were problematic. The rest qualified as motorcycle clubs, whose only interest was hanging out together and showing off their bikes.

Dixie had respect for motorcycles. She'd ridden herself a few years ago. Had a boyfriend in the Marines who took her lots of places, before he shipped out to Okinawa and they lost contact.

Once the sound of engines completely died down, people began to move on the streets. In unspoken agreement, they avoided walking close to the side of the street where the motorcycles had parked. Dixie observed for a moment and then made her way to the library. *I'll check into that later.*

She walked inside and stopped. *Wow, did I conjure this woman?*

Sure enough, the exact person she expected to be standing behind the library counter was actually...standing behind the library counter. A woman in her fifties, wearing a denim jumper and white shirt, stared at her computer screen. Her long gray hair had been pulled back in a braid. She wore half glasses perched at the end of her nose.

Dixie walked toward the counter, waiting to be noticed. Finally the woman turned her way. "Can I help you?" she asked, her bright eyes taking in Dixie's appearance. "A visitor to Lily Rock?"

How the devil did she know that? I look like everyone else. Jeans and a t-shirt and scuffed boots. "Yah, I'm a visitor," she admitted, knowing it was useless to argue. "I was wondering if you could help me find a place to stay for a couple of days?"

The woman walked closer. "Your name?" she asked.

Without thinking, she began to speak her real name. Stopping immediately, lest she give away her cover, she sputtered something unintelligible. Once she'd gained her composure she answered, "Dixie Jones. And yours?"

"I'm Meadow McCloud."

"You're the Lily Rock librarian?"

"That's right, dear. The one and only. So you came up the hill without a reservation? This is Christmastime and everything will be full until after New Year's."

She felt herself bristle. But because Meadow McCloud looked so pleasant, she deliberately shifted her tone of voice. "I had a reservation but that doesn't seem to count much around here. Taking a break from insurance, just for the holidays. Long story short? I don't have a place to stay. A mistake."

"I see." The woman nodded, her face softening. "Are you alone?"

"Yes, I am." Dixie felt uncomfortable and strangely saddened. So she tightened her chin so as not to give away any vulnerability. "I am alone," she repeated more for herself. "I like it that way," she added, as if she needed to explain.

Meadow smiled. "You look like a good person to me. Why don't you stay at my house this weekend? I live just outside the center of town and have a spare room with a bathroom nearby."

When Dixie began to shake her head in protest, the woman kept talking. "My daughter, Sage, won't be home from school for another couple of days. Winter break doesn't begin until after finals. So it would be just the two of us."

Dixie stared. *Is this woman for real? She doesn't even know me and she's invited me to spend the night. I could be a serial killer.*

Meadow leaned her elbows on the counter. "Do you really

have a choice, dear? If you want to spend the night, this may be your only option."

The sheer practicality of her words struck Dixie as solid. "You're right. Beggars can't be choosers, now can they?"

"That's what my mother would have said." Meadow smirked. "But I can assure you my hospitality is renowned in Lily Rock. You won't be begging for anything."

Dixie knew she should apologize. But before she opened her mouth, Meadow shoved a piece of paper across the counter. "Here's my address. Like I said I'm right outside of town. Spend some time looking at the books or walk around for a bit. I'll be done here in an hour and I'll meet you at my house."

She considered her situation. *I guess this could work in my favor. I could learn a lot about Lily Rock and get my assignment finished faster if I stay with her. She seems pretty smart. Except for opening her house to a complete stranger, something that's just not safe. But I suppose we could get along.*

"Okay, see you later." She took the paper. "I will take a look around the library if you don't mind. Any public computers?"

"Right over there behind the sofa," the librarian whispered. Then she turned back to her desk.

Dixie scanned the room. She found an overstuffed sofa in the middle of the library, the stacks filling the spaces to the sides and behind. Three people sat side by side reading books. Behind the sofa was a long table holding three computers. They were all occupied.

I don't think I can ease in on the people at the computers without drawing unnecessary attention to myself. She changed her mind. Instead of remaining in the library, she walked out the door toward the boardwalk. Dixie stopped and then shook her head, wondering about the strange rise of emotion when she'd been talking to Meadow.

She'd admitted to the friendly librarian that she was alone. Her bottom lip had begun to tremble. *Look at me, getting all emotional. I hate it when that happens.*

Making a mental note of the motorcycles still parked in Lola's lot, she heard music blaring from inside the business. "Born to be Wild" by Steppenwolf. *They must have outdoor speakers. Surprising considering the small-town vibe is probably a selling point for all of the small businesses. I'd expect "Frosty the Snowman" and "Jingle Bells".*

Leaving the folksy side of the street with the cutesy signs and gingerbread exteriors, she stepped off the curb. *This may be exactly what I'm here for. To drive the bikers out of town...* She'd not read the anonymous email herself but had taken the captain's word for it.

She took a deep breath, appreciating the scent of pine. Hugging her arms around her middle, she wondered if she'd packed warm enough clothing in her small suitcase.

I have that old leather jacket in the back of my car. At least I'll fit in with the bikers. I can go over there this evening after I find Meadow's house. She walked toward her vehicle, picking up the pace to stay warm.

4

WELL SEASONED

"You're never gonna believe this, Captain. I'm unpacked already. Got a room with the Lily Rock librarian. Her name is Meadow McCloud. Her daughter is called Sage. Geez, I'm so over the nature names. Never mind."

"Anyway, I put on a sad face and Meadow just up and invited me to stay at her place. She didn't even ask many questions. Just my name. I told her I'm in insurance. I kind of am. Not a total lie, I mean policing is a kind of insurance, is it not?"

She took a quick breath, diving back into her monologue before he could interrupt. "In any case, I'm in the spare bedroom. You're not gonna believe this. Lace curtains and doilies. Everywhere. I bet Meadow crocheted them herself."

"Stop talking!" barked the captain.

Dixie shut her mouth, remembering Brian's warning. "Sorry, sir. I'm a little overly excited. My first undercover assignment." *I wonder which part he didn't like. The free room or the doilies?* Before he could speak, she heard a knock on the door.

"Yah?" Dixie responded.

Meadow stuck her head inside the room. "Am I disturbing

you, dear?" She cast a disapproving glance at Dixie, who sat against the headboard, her shoes on the pristine chenille comforter.

"Hold on," Dixie told the captain. Slipping her feet over the edge, she stood up to greet Meadow. "I'm on the phone for work," she explained. *Now go away and crochet a doily and leave me alone.*

"You're invited to a grill fest in the backyard at six." Meadow looked down at Dixie's worn boots. "Wear something comfortable. I've left a towel in the bathroom in case you want to tidy up."

"I'd love to come." Dixie didn't have to feign enthusiasm. *Lola's can wait. This investigation is falling right into my lap. I can eat a burger and meet some Lily Rock residents all in one night. I haven't been here for a day and the investigation is practically over. Yay me!*

"See you in the backyard around six." Meadow closed the door softly behind her.

"Still there, Captain? Did you hear that? Our local librarian is marching Lily Rock residents before me, like lambs to the slaughter. I should be able to wrap this up tomorrow."

Dixie sat back on the bed, her shoes still on. In a quick glance around the room, she noted the dresser with the mirror hung on the wall above. The curtains with the crochet edges, and the doily on the bedside table. *My grandma would have loved this place.*

"Uh-huh," she said into the phone. "Great advice. Gotta go." She waited for him to say goodbye first. *I've got a few minutes to take a shower before the...what did she call it? A grill fest? Please. Pretentious much? I bet she provided a small soap and a shower cap for my convenience.* Dixie chuckled, feeling very good about herself.

Twenty minutes later, showered and ready, she pulled on

her spare pair of jeans. She'd packed her fancy wool sweater for a night out, or in case she met an attractive man to hang out with, should the prospect turn up. *You never know. Lily Rock may include a sexy cowboy.* At least that's what she told herself when she'd packed earlier that day.

The sweater felt warm and soft against her skin. She ran her hand down the front, feeling the silky wool under her fingers. Bending her neck over, she lifted the hair off her neck. Damp but not soaking, she ran her fingers through her curls. Then she flipped her head back to look at herself in the mirror. Out of the usual tight bun at the back of her neck, her hair tumbled to her shoulders. With a few twists around her finger, she made corkscrew curls around her face. *Lookin' good, Dixie Jones.*

Closing the door softly behind her, she stood in the hallway. Voices came from the living room. Rather than bust in on them and stop the casual repartee, she paused to listen. One man spoke at great length. *Why do men with deep bass voices like to talk so much?* Taking a few steps closer, she hesitated again, hoping to hear more of the conversation.

"Oh Doc, you're incorrigible," came a woman's soft slur.

Laughter followed until Meadow spoke up. "I have a guest for all of you to meet."

On cue Dixie hurried down the rest of the hallway to make an entrance in the living room. Heads turned toward her. The older man with the thick silver hair smiled appreciatively. Next to him stood a woman, one whose fit body had been poured into a tight red top with black skinny jeans. She looked like a woman who made a real effort with her appearance. Her age still showed, around sixty.

The woman nodded slightly in Dixie's direction.

The man stepped forward, his eyes focused on the front of Dixie's sweater like she was a fine drawing and he an art expert. His hand reached out. "I'm Callahan May. Lily Rock's doctor," he added with a slight smile.

Well, aren't you the old gray fox?

She grasped his hand. Gave it a strong grip. And then dropped it. His eyes narrowed. *Don't like it when a lady takes charge, do you, old codger.* And because she couldn't help herself, she said aloud, "Don't like doctors much. They think they have all the answers."

"But they do," piped the woman, "have all the answers. Especially this man." She looked up at Callahan May with her most seductive grin. After a slight pause, she turned to Dixie, extending her hand, palm down. A large topaz ring sat on her middle finger.

Why do I feel like I'm supposed to kiss her ring? It's the smooth jazz voice and the way she offered it...

Dixie reached out and shook the woman's hand vigorously.

"I'm Doc's receptionist and nurse," she explained, still not giving up her name.

She thinks I'm supposed to know who she is. Okay then, Miss Entitled 1965. The woman stepped closer, easing her way between Dixie and the doctor and blocking his stare. *She's not giving him a chance to say more. Those two might be a couple.*

Dixie took a step to the side as she looked past the woman. The doc smiled knowingly. Her eyes narrowed, and then she broke eye contact with him to look back at the woman. "So I know what your job is, but you didn't tell me your name."

"I'm Skye Jones," she said. "And you are?"

"Dixie Jones."

"Are we related?" The woman's eyes grew round. *Like she hasn't met another Jones before. Note to self: I will pick a name other than Jones the next time I go undercover. Common is one thing, overused could be a problem.*

"Not that I know of." Dixie brushed her off with her firm voice, which usually worked with overly friendly people who used small talk to get information.

Meadow called out, "Arlo and Michael are outside. Why don't we join them?"

The doc went first, followed by Skye. Dixie waited for Meadow. "Are these your neighbors?"

"We are neighbors but also a committee," Meadow explained.

"So this is a town meeting then?"

"We informally run the town, like a council. We're planning the Christmas Eve event. The tree lighting is coming up. Snow is predicted, so we need to get moving. It's quite the big deal here. I hope you'll be able to stay for the tree lighting. It's on the twenty-fourth."

Dixie smiled politely. It took a lot of effort. She wondered if her lips would freeze in that position. They felt dry.

"Oh, I'll be gone by then. Plus I don't do Christmas. Not Santa, not Jesus."

Meadow's eyebrows raised. "I suppose that makes some sense. But just so you know, no one does Christmas. Christmas does you. It either happens in your heart or it doesn't. Not your decision to make." As if pleased with dispensing her own wisdom, Meadow smiled.

Oh geez. Not this. A God-fearing woman with an agenda. God help me. Dixie glanced up toward the ceiling. *No, that wasn't a prayer. Just a request to an unknown deity.* She quickly brought down her gaze, rolling her eyes at Meadow, who watched her face with interest.

"Why don't you go first." Meadow swept her hand toward the kitchen. "Out the back door where I've set the table."

Dixie walked into the kitchen, past the long table to open the back door. Her eyes took in the scene. People standing with drinks in their hands and... *Who do we have here?*

A man hovered over the grill, his profile showing a firm jawline and a strong athletic body. *Well, look at you, tall, dark, and handsome. Welcome to Lily Rock, Dixie Jones.*

He glanced at her out of the corner of his eye. A smile started at the corner of his mouth, working its way down to his generous lips. Standing over six feet tall, his shoulders filled out a soft flannel shirt. A quilted gray vest, worn over rolled-up sleeves, exposed strong forearms and tanned skin. His hair looked clean. Not too short, brushed back off his face.

He waved a spatula in the air. "You must be Dixie Jones. Meadow said you were staying with her." His grin widened, his voice filled with unspoken expectation. "I'm the chef for tonight. How would you like your steak?"

Dixie gulped. "Well seasoned," she said. And then paused for effect before adding, "Just like my men."

TALL, DARK, AND HANDSOME

Two bites into the perfect T-bone, Dixie sat back in her chair. *Grill master and great-looking.* Her mouth watered. *Hello Lily Rock.*

She pretended to cut away another bite of steak, but her eyes drifted toward the grill. When he stopped chatting with the doc and Skye, she dabbed at her lips, readying herself for his approach.

Holding a plate with steak, baked potato, and broccoli, he nodded to the table. "Mind if I join you?" he asked.

"I'd expect nothing less," she said brightly. "I didn't catch your name."

He folded his well-built frame into the chair across from hers, placing the plate in front of him on the table. "Michael Bellemare," he answered.

"Don't tell me you are a permanent Lily Rock resident," Dixie scoffed. "It doesn't seem like your kind of place."

"What do you think my kind of place would look like?" His eyebrows raised.

Proud of her ability to size people up, she jumped right in. "You're big city. Probably New York or Chicago. You make yourself comfortable wherever you go, but your home isn't here in this small town."

Mild surprise crossed his face. "And you're not an insurance person either," he said, watching her for a response.

She glared back at him. *I'm not going to defend my cover. I don't want to blurt out unnecessary lies that I have to remember later.* She poked at the meat to give herself time to reassess. "I've done some work in insurance. But I'm here for other reasons." She'd gotten good at telling partial truths. She'd learned this technique at the academy, while interviewing suspects who asked too many questions.

"I believe you." Without further comment he cut into his steak. It oozed blood.

"You have a deft skill when it comes to grilling," she said dryly.

He chewed as if thinking of a response. When he raised his eyebrows again, she giggled. *Get your flirt on, Dixie. Now reel him in.*

He gazed at her, his eyes warm, his expression open. He kept his glance to her eyes and mouth. *Go ahead. Look at my chest. I'm rocking this tight sweater. Go ahead. Then I know that you want what I want, nothin' more. No long-term commitment or presents on your birthday. Unless of course today is your birthday...*

When he cut another piece of meat and still hadn't spoken, she tried again. "I saw a bar in town earlier. Called Lola's. You know anything about that place?" *Take my cue. Now you can ask me out for a drink.*

He took a bite of baked potato. "I'm here on business as well, and I've got a commitment tomorrow morning. A rich woman found my name in an architectural journal and then asked me to design her house. Plans are finished and permits set. We're ready to break ground."

So no drink at Lola's. She hid her disappointment by turning her face down to her plate again. With Lola's off the table for tonight, she asked another pointed question.

"Meadow said this was a committee grill night. If you're not a full-time resident, how did you get invited?"

"It's been a year since I moved to Lily Rock for this job. One thing led to another. I met a few people. I had no intention of getting involved in the town politics, but I had problems getting building permits through their system. Without an official town council, I had to court a group called the Old Rockers."

"Just heard about them."

"My design isn't..." He paused and swallowed.

He looks surprised. Maybe he doesn't usually talk that much to strange women. That's because he's putty in my interviewing hands. She sent him a go-on look.

"Let's just say my design is not that usual in Lily Rock. It's taken longer than I'm used to just to get this project up and running."

Before she could ask another question, a man approached. "Am I intruding on your conversation? he asked.

"Have a seat, Arlo," Michael said. "Meet Dixie Jones. She's here on business." He winked at her.

"I'm in insurance," she quickly added.

Arlo chuckled. He pulled a chair over, then set his plate next to Michael's. "I don't need insurance. My husband handles all of our finances."

"Except for the new pub," Michael corrected him.

Arlo nodded. "That's true. I'm responsible for all aspects of the new brew pub. I answer to Doc, even about the construction of the new building."

"Did I hear my name?" The doctor came closer to their table. Dixie was aware that he'd been listening to their conversation. He came up next to her, and she felt the heat of his body at her back. When he touched her shoulder in greeting, she shrugged him off.

"On the subject of bars. I saw Lola's. Will your new brew pub be cutting into their business?"

When no one answered her, she tried again. "Why don't you take over Lola's instead of building an entirely new structure?"

Doc patted her shoulder, apparently unfazed by her rebuff. "You don't know Lily Rock, my dear. Arlo and I see great potential in a brew pub. It's taken a while but now that Michael Bellemare, the famous Chicago architect, is in town, we thought we'd hire him to create a design that would bring younger, more hip tourists up the hill."

"And serve the people who already live here," Arlo added. "They're welcome too."

"Maybe Lola's will go out of business." Dixie watched Arlo's and Doc's faces to see if she'd figured out their unspoken plan.

Bingo. Arlo was the first to look uncomfortable. "Doc is the only Old Rocker who sees how Lily Rock is changing. He and I have a vision for what the place could be. Lola's doesn't have to go. They serve a different clientele."

So they want to bring new people up the hill with a brew pub, but I wonder if they want police presence as well... That may be the rift that's caused the anonymous requests for police presence.

She turned her gaze to Michael. "So you are a big city famous guy. I knew you weren't from here."

A slight flush rose up his neck. He lifted his hand to brush back a stray piece of hair that had fallen over his eye. "I guess I am famous. To some people. But it's my father who runs the architectural firm. I'm a little splash, he's the tsunami."

Oh stop. Humble too. This guy is too much. She took inventory of each man's face again. *I think I've asked enough questions for now.*

"I'll be right back." Dixie stood to her feet and walked around the table to dump her plate in the trash. She came back to the table, leaning over to whisper in Michael's ear. She thrust her cell phone into his hand and said, "Put your number in my contacts and I'll text you so you'll have my number too. That way you can call me before I leave town."

He took her phone, a sheepish grin on his face. He added his number and handed it back to her.

"Merry Christmas, Michael Bellemare," she said, sliding the phone into her back pocket. On her way toward the kitchen, she heard Dr. May's voice call out, "Do you want my number?"

"I'm good," she hollered back.

Once inside the kitchen she found Skye and Meadow sitting at the oversized table. Meadow rubbed her temples with both hands. "I hope you liked the food," she said. "Planning for the tree lighting is getting rather hectic."

"We're missing an important decoration for the ceremony tomorrow," Skye explained.

"Hopefully not the lights," Dixie added brightly.

"No, dear," Meadow said. "We're missing the baby Jesus. I usually store our life-sized figurine in the shed out back, with the creche and the statues of the wise people and the shepherds."

"Wise people? I thought they were men."

"Oh, we're very open-minded when it comes to gender identity in Lily Rock," Meadow explained offhandedly.

Who do you think you are, Los Angeles? She looked back and forth and concluded aloud, "No baby Jesus. Maybe you'll have to cancel the event."

Skye glared at her. "We formed a committee to search for the baby. If that doesn't work we can always bundle up a bunch of hay, wrap it in a blanket. It's just a shame we can't find the old statue. It looked at lot like Sage when she was a baby. That sweet smile."

Meadow nodded her agreement.

"Must be a sentimental loss. I get that."

"Yes, it is. But things change." Meadow sighed deeply.

"Maybe we need more police protection now that Lily Rock has gotten so big." Skye looked at Meadow as if asking for an affirmation.

Meadow quickly said, "No police. The Old Rockers still handle things. We're not giving up our privacy because someone misplaced an old ceramic baby Jesus."

Bingo. Maybe it's Skye who sent the request for police presence. She seems more concerned about crime than Meadow.

* * *

Later that night, when Dixie returned to her room, she reported to the captain about what she'd learned.

He explained more about the emails. "It's not just a missing statue. Someone has been sending in reports about other things, more sinister suspicions. Drugging animals at the local shelter. And then the presence of bikers every weekend. Have you looked into any of those problems?"

"I did see the bikers." Stifling a yawn, Dixie rolled over in bed, keeping the cell next to her ear. "I tried to bring up Lola's at dinner, but the men didn't bite. Told me about a plan for a new brew pub. There was some mention of serving a different clientele, but no direct comment about the bikers."

"One more day, Dixie Jones!" the captain barked. "Then you're back with a full report."

"Yes, sir." She stifled another yawn.

Once she set her phone on the nightstand, she rolled on her back and closed her eyes. Then she opened her eyes with a start. A quick glance at her phone brought a sigh. *No messages.*

Everyone else calls him Michael. Not me. Tonight I'm going to be dreaming of Mike Bellemare. Mr. Tall, Dark, and Handsome...

6

ANOTHER ANONYMOUS EMAIL

Dixie lay in her bed, curled into a ball. She sniffed. *Lavender. Definitely still in Kansas.* Opening her eyes, she groaned. A ray of sun shot through the curtains over her bed.

She sat up straight, swinging her feet out from under the covers. She reached for her phone and then tapped her screen to check the time.

It's after nine o'clock!

Her heart raced. But instead of hurrying, she yawned and lay back against the pillows, pulling her feet back up onto the bed. Dixie brought the phone closer, thumbing through her messages. Three calls from the captain and a text from Michael Bellemare.

Mike. I knew you'd text. She'd felt their connection, remembered the way his eyes sparked as she peppered him with one pointed question after the next.

She also liked how the muscles on his upper arms could be seen under the fabric of his flannel shirt. Oh, and how he smiled and joked and didn't take her quite so seriously.

Swinging her legs over the side of the bed again, she put her feet on the floor as she read the text once more.

How about I show you my latest project? I'll text later with a time. An emoji with fingers crossed made her smile. *Yep, we connected. But only one more day in Lily Rock to hook up.*

She liked one-night stands. That kept her out of the emotional quagmire of relationship dramas. Her job was her one true passion, or at least that was what she told herself.

In no hurry, Dixie composed the perfect response to his text. She picked a gif of a group of *Seinfeld* actors dancing wildly. She added, Okay. And then she pushed Send. The *swish* sound made her feel happy.

By the time she'd dressed and left her room, she felt refreshed and ready for a new day. She followed the coffee aroma through the living room into the kitchen. Someone had left a key on the table with a note tucked under the edge of a wooden box marked "Bread". She read the note.

"Here's the house key. The kitchen is yours."

Dixie stuffed the key into her jeans pocket, then walked to the counter. A full carafe huddled together with an empty mug. She picked up the carafe to pour coffee into the mug. Steam escaped along with the strong smell of a French roast.

"Isn't Meadow the hostess with the mostest," Dixie mumbled. She looked around as she sipped coffee. Her stomach grumbled. She turned toward the table. *Maybe a slice of bread?*

She eyed the wooden box. Once open she got more than she bargained for. A loaf slightly warm to the touch lay alongside a butter dish and a knife. The butter felt soft and ready to spread.

She lifted the loaf like a prize and held it to her nose. Her mouth watered. *Why am I so happy about bread...* She took the knife and lay the bread on the butcher block tabletop. Slicing two thick pieces, she returned the rest of the loaf to the box.

Butter first. Once she slathered on the butter, she turned toward the refrigerator.

A search revealed a glass container labeled "Strawberry jam". *Looks homemade.* Dixie shoved the door closed. She took the jam to the table and sat down to spread a thin layer on top of the butter. First she took a sip of coffee and then eagerly bit into her breakfast.

* * *

Standing outside the front door, Dixie paused. She usually rushed out in the morning, eager to continue her academy training. But today she felt no hurry. It had been a long time since she'd been this relaxed. *It must be the mountain air.* She looked up. The sky had become overcast and the temperature had dropped. She pulled her jacket around her shoulders before closing the front door behind her, walking down the driveway toward her car.

She held her breath for a moment. *I need to appreciate this clean air. Live in the moment. My new motto.*

Sliding into the driver's seat, she remembered. *I didn't call the captain back.* She hit redial and waited.

"Where have you been?" came his demanding voice.

"I slept in. Part of my backstory. Dixie Jones is a late riser."

"Don't give me that."

Boy, he's in a bad mood. Then it occurred to her in a snippet, a brief brain flash. *He's always in a bad mood. I just stopped noticing.*

"We've had another anonymous email from Lily Rock," he barked.

Have you now. From the librarian who hands out house keys to strangers, or the nurse receptionist who I suspect is in love with the town doctor? Maybe the architect who grills a mean steak has sent you a message...

"Yes, sir." *Stay back, bad attitude.*

"What kind of surveillance are you running there?" came his suspicious voice.

"Just doing my job, sir," she replied sweetly.

"You didn't give a full report of the architect last night. Is he of interest? An out-of-town guy is a good disguise for someone running drugs."

Dixie felt her gut clench. "He's famous. Name is Bellemare. He's hardly a crook."

"And you know that because..."

"Because I have a date with him later today. Strictly undercover work." She wanted to make sure the captain knew it wasn't personal, even though it felt personal. Lying about her emotions had become second nature. The truth was she hadn't been able to stop thinking about Mike since last night.

"Gonna have a little fun before you leave Lily Rock?" the captain snarled.

She cleared her throat. "I thought you were going to tell me about the latest anonymous email."

"Someone has vandalized the storage unit where they keep the props. Everyone is looking for the missing item."

"Is this about the missing baby Jesus?"

"Yes, it is," he continued. "Someone in town thought it important enough to email the police. Like I said, maybe the search is important. Why don't you join the search committee today and see what you can uncover?"

"I'm on it. I plan on being there when they set up this morning to eavesdrop on conversations. Plus they probably just misplaced the figurine. It'll turn up."

"See who looks the most likely to be sending those anonymous emails. Then we can interview them and get to the bottom of this."

"Yes, sir."

"Bikers, brew pubs, and break-ins. Stay focused," he added.

"Don't worry, Captain. I'm gonna be ever so helpful today. I'll make myself useful and snoop around while they're setting up the Christmas shebang to see what I can find out."

"Right. Hope your date goes well."

Did she detect a leer in his voice...

Before she could tell him to mind his own business, the captain ended the conversation. "Gotta go. Someone's on my other phone line."

Dixie didn't believe him for a minute. But she was happy to hang up.

7

THE SET UP

Dixie drove slowly down the mountain road toward town. Her mind shifted back and forth, flitting from thoughts of Michael Bellemare to her impatience with small towns, Lily Rock in particular. *Missing baby Jesus. Please. I am not a cop in a Hallmark movie.*

The memory of Meadow's homemade bread with butter and jam also unsettled her opinions. *I'm not a foodie. Since when do I care about bread and butter?* Her mouth watered as she cautioned herself. *Don't get so involved. Maybe a small-town job is a bad idea for me. I may change my mind and ask for the valley instead.*

It must be the clean air making me feel vulnerable. I need more smog!

It was her habit to distance herself from her feelings. She had what she called her I-don't-care mantra. Repeating "I don't care" over and over. "I don't care," she said aloud in the car, "about clean mountain air." *And now I'm rhyming?* Defeated by her own mantra, she glanced to the side of the road, trying again. "I don't care about squirrels with fluffy tails or trees that smell like Christmas every day." Swerving into a curve, she had to brake quickly so as not to skid.

As she righted the car her glance drifted out the windshield. Her eyes widened as she took in the rugged mountainside in the distance. One large rock formation stood out against the rest. It shimmered in the morning sun. "I also don't care about the view and that oversized boulder they call Lily Rock," she said aloud.

She swerved into the next curve. For the first time she questioned her attraction to Mike Bellemare. *I don't care about smart, dark, and handsome Mike Bellemare. What kind of a fancy name is that?* She slowed her vehicle down. A truck, overloaded with boxes, had come to a halt in front of her. She freaked suddenly, watching as a box in front of her teetered over, spilling out the contents. A plastic reindeer and a sleigh stared over the tailgate.

She blinked. The deer peered directly at her. "Stop staring at me," Dixie groaned. *And why am I talking to statues all of a sudden...*

When the truck ahead didn't budge, she pressed the palm of her hand against the car horn. Tapping her fingers on the steering wheel, she reached across to the passenger seat to grab her phone. *Mike hasn't texted me about what time he wants to meet up.* Her finger raised to send another text, but she stopped herself. *What are you doing?* She tossed the phone back on the seat just as the tail lights on the truck ahead blinked off and on.

She took her foot from the brake, accelerating forward and around the stopped truck. She slammed on the brake again; her eyes caught a problem by the side of the road. A family of four—mom, dad, and two small children—stood near the cliff, backs to the view of Lily Rock.

The mother held a phone in front of her to take a family

selfie. Dixie inched her car to the side of the road as the cars behind her beeped. She rolled down the passenger window to holler.

"Look out for the drop," she called loudly. The mother put down her phone as the father's face registered the intensity of her tone.

"Come on, kids." He immediately ushered the family away from the drop-off.

Relieved that they were out of danger, Dixie shook her head and quickly pulled back into traffic. She drove fifteen miles per hour until she made it into town.

She pulled into the first parking space she could find and turned off the ignition, leaving her vehicle behind to stand on the boardwalk. Despite the cooling temperatures, the sun shone brightly over the center of town, where a gaggle of people waited, talking to one another.

Some held strings of lights, which fell from their hands to the dirt in disarray. A long orange extension cord lay on the dirt, plugged into an outlet close to Lola's entrance. Dixie watched as one man dropped his string of lights, trying to untangle them using both hands. Others watched.

"We're setting up for tomorrow's tree lighting." Skye Jones appeared at Dixie's side. She looked trim, dressed in denim jeans and worn boots, appearing more like a mountain woman than a nurse.

"I could give a hand. You know I'm only going to be here for another day, so might as well make myself useful." *Look at me quoting the captain.*

Skye looked her up and down. "That would be nice. Just so you know, Michael won't be here today. He's at work on Marla's place. They're a couple. He's taken."

Dixie held her expression steady, not wanting Skye to know she'd hit a raw nerve. She didn't want to expose her disappointment. So she stared right back at the woman, her chin set. "I can still help with the setup," she offered again, mostly to cover up her embarrassment.

"Okay then, just so you know what's what. Come with me. I'll take you to Arlo and he can give you an assignment. Maybe untangling the strings and testing the rest of the lights..."

She followed Skye across the street. *So Mike's in a relationship. But he seemed so into me last night.* She swallowed back her disappointment. *Maybe it was the Lily Rock pixie dust. I let my guard down.*

Dixie spotted Arlo right away. He stood in the middle of Lola's parking lot. Her friend, the plastic deer, lay in the dirt behind a car's bumper. *I guess that guy dumped him and drove away.*

Yesterday the motorcycles had caught her attention. Today it was the shrubbery that piqued her interest. All around the perimeter of the dirt parking lot were overgrown dead bushes. Weeds dangled from crunchy stems, most likely dried from the summer heat. Thick dry brush surrounded the foundation of Lola's, not a green twig in sight.

Dixie sighed. She noted bales of straw stacked against the wood siding of the bar, making her feel even more uneasy. *Straw only makes this a fire waiting to happen. I hope it snows sooner rather than later.*

Next to the straw for the nativity, she glimpsed a gaudy plastic statue of a man. *Probably Joseph.* Molded feet in the air, the head had been shoved into the dirt. Next to him was a woman in a blue cloak. She lay on the ground, her scratched painted face pointing upward. Next to her were two shepherds holding crooks, painted to look like they'd come from the desert. Headdresses hung around their faces.

Dixie walked closer to look at the statues. One shepherd's

feet stuck up in the air. Encased in sandals, the paint had chipped away. One big toe was missing.

"That's the holy family, right?" Skye called to Dixie.

"I think so," Dixie said, looking confused.

"Are you Christian?" came Skye's next question.

"Nope. Are you Jewish...or do you celebrate Kwanzaa?" Dixie turned the questions back at Skye.

"I thought Kwanzaa was for African Americans," Skye retorted. Then she added, "Lily Rock celebrates all the faith traditions."

"I don't see any Ramadan representation," Dixie quickly challenged.

Skye snapped, "I got a 'Happy Ramadan' flag at Walmart last year. You'll find it in one of those boxes." She pointed to a stack of cardboard containers that had been tossed to the ground. A Santa had fallen free of one box, his nose in the dust next to a now familiar sight: Dixie's plastic reindeer.

She repressed a smile. "So you're taking on all the traditions, not just Christmas. Very egalitarian of you. Inclusive. Actually bland, if you want to know my real opinion. Why don't you Lily Rock people just stick to your own traditions instead of including every Tom, Dick, and Harry?"

Skye glared at Dixie. "I hope you don't express that opinion to Meadow. She may kick you right out of your free lodging. Now go over there and see if you can make yourself useful. I have to meet with Doc."

"I bet you do," Dixie muttered. *I bet you've been meeting with Doc for years now, as his nurse and sexy-time partner.* She spotted Arlo and walked toward him, brushing off her irritation with Skye before she said too much.

"Hey, it's you," Arlo remarked as soon as he saw her. "Here to help?"

"I am," she said.

"Why don't you go over there? It's time to stake out the holy family. Can you use a hammer?"

She glared at him. "When necessary."

"Okay then, get some tools and follow the people who are placing the statues in the dirt. As soon as they're done you can start digging and hammering the stakes around the base of each figure."

"Why are you in charge of all of this?" She glanced around, not succeeding in sounding anything other than sarcastic.

"I just follow orders from the Old Rockers," he explained.

"An old what?" She played stupid, hoping he'd divulge more information.

"We don't have an official town council. The people who've lived on the hill call themselves Old Rockers. Meadow, Skye, Doc. My husband, Cay, and I have been here over five years but that doesn't make us Old Rockers."

Arlo nodded toward Lola's. "Old man Maguire is also an Old Rocker. That's why we put the displays in his open lot. He gives us the electricity for free. You'll see him around. Kind of stooped over, bald skinny guy."

Before she could ask more, Arlo moved away. "See you later," he said over his shoulder.

She edged closer to the statues lying in the dirt. Meadow held a fake sheep in her arms. "Put Joseph and Mary here where the creche will be. Here's a shovel." Meadow pointed with her foot and then kept instructing. "Get a bucket and wash Joseph and Mary first. They look terrible with all that dirt on their faces."

"Still no baby Jesus?" Dixie noticed aloud.

"Until we find where he's stored, we'll use bundled hay in a blanket. But by tomorrow the children will expect to see the baby in the manger. If he hasn't turned up by then, we could find a dolly at the thrift store. I hate to disappoint anyone, especially the children."

"I've experienced a recent disappointment," Dixie said, surprised she was willing to mention it to Meadow. "It's no fun." Her thoughts went back to Mike and then to Skye. "Kids don't really care about the baby in the manger. They just want presents."

Meadow held the sheep to her chest as her eyes softened. "You sound as if you need a good old-fashioned Lily Rock Christmas. I hope the tree lighting will get you in the holiday spirit."

Fat chance. I haven't been in a holiday mood for at least a decade.

Dixie bent over to pick up the bucket and a spray bottle filled with water. *Look out, Joseph and Mary. Time for a spray and wash.*

8

TOO MUCH TOUCHY-FEELY

Dixie stood back with Arlo, Skye, and Meadow to assess the progress of the holiday installation.

"We've got the menorah over there." Arlo nodded.

"Each tradition has its own location," Meadow explained to her. "I hope someone finds the baby Jesus before tomorrow night."

Dixie smirked. "You've got wise men, two plastic sheep, and that other thing."

"It's a camel," Meadow said.

"It's seen some wear." Arlo grinned.

"What happens next?" Dixie wondered out loud.

"The lights." Arlo glanced upward. "The crane will be here soon. He got caught behind traffic coming up the hill."

Meadow looked down at her feet and nudged a large root growing up out of the packed dirt. "We really have to do something about these roots above the surface."

Arlo glanced down to her boot. "The roots aren't healthy," he agreed. "People walking over them doesn't help."

"The trees are dying," Skye added.

"Yet you continue to put lights on them," said Dixie.

Meadow turned to her. "We've run into a quandary. Our traditions and the dry climate. The Old Rockers have been discussing this problem for the past five years.

"Maguire," she continued, nodding toward the bar, "is generous when it comes to celebrating the holidays on his land. We turn a blind eye to some of his less desirable clientele just to keep him happy."

"The problem is," Arlo added, "less and less precipitation and then parking motorcycles and driving stakes into the earth around those sequoias is disrupting the ecosystem. Something has to change or we will lose those giant trees."

"That would be horrible," admitted Skye.

Dixie kept quiet, but she wanted to tell them what to do. To her it seemed obvious. Hadn't she just learned they'd designed a new brew pub? They could demolish the ramshackle bar or move it somewhere else. Bring in a sequoia expert and then heal the trees.

Straightforward thoughts like this often got Dixie into trouble at the academy. To avoid ridicule, she'd learned to keep most of her thoughts to herself. *Plus I'm not here to fix Lily Rock, just observe and make a report.*

Her phone buzzed. She reached into her pocket and found that it was a text from Michael Bellemare.

Still on?

She thought for a moment. Now that she knew he had a girlfriend, she wasn't sure that a meetup with him would help her investigation. The memory of his quick smile came to mind.

She texted back. I'm busy.

I'll come get you.

She started to text him more details about her location but then stopped. She shoved the phone into her back pocket. "I'm hungry," she told them and then pointed across the street to a sign that read Lily Rock Diner. "Going to get a bite to eat over there. See you later."

There was nothing Dixie Jones liked more than a quick and efficient exit. She made it a habit to keep people guessing. Plus the groupthink in Lily Rock made her queasy. *It's like they all know what the other one thinks and feels. A playground for disaster if you ask me. Too much touchy-feely and not enough honest disagreement.*

A small group of nefarious villains could take over a town like this. Drugs would be dealt, people trafficked, others bullied into keeping quiet. Next thing you know, Lily Rock could become a town with everyone carrying a weapon and no one admitting there's a problem.

She thought of the bikers that pulled into town the day before and shuddered.

* * *

A seat at the counter was empty. Dixie nodded to the waitress, who held a small pad of paper in her hand. Spinning the stool around a couple of times she sat down facing the counter.

Over her shoulder she noted an exit with a restroom sign above the door. A black and white photo of Santa hung on the wall, as if in a place of honor. She recognized the lift of his chin even behind the fake beard.

I bet that's Doc May back in the day.

A shelf had been constructed around the room, two feet from the ceiling. Tinsel dangled from the edges, along with green swags and ball-shaped decorations in red, white, and blue.

She sniffed. *The decorations are a bit much, but the*

burgers smell great... I like this place. Without even glancing at the menu Dixie knew just what to order.

"A burger with fries and a chocolate milkshake," she told the waitress, who wore a navy-blue apron tied around her waist.

"Here or to go?"

"Oh definitely here. You worked at this place long?"

"'Bout twenty years," she said brightly. "You want water too? I can add some lemon."

Dixie grinned. "Water no lemon would be great."

As the waitress turned to go, Dixie made it her business to glance at the people on either side of her. One man hovered over his chili, arms on the counter, shoveling piles of his food into his mouth. The guy on her right had spun his stool to face the man on his right, his back to Dixie. She didn't take offense. *Diner etiquette for mind your own business.*

Boundaries. Diners are my place. Where I feel at home. For the first time since she'd driven into Lily Rock, she let her guard down.

When she finished her burger and the last fry, she took a sip of water and then pushed away her plate to pull the milkshake closer. A bell sounded over the door. She took a long sip of the shake, savoring the cool goodness slipping down her throat.

"Thought I'd find you here," came his warm deep voice.

Dixie knew who it was. She kept her eyes on the straw, willing her body to calm down before she acknowledged his presence. Taking her time, she swallowed and then picked up the half-empty glass. Turning the stool toward him, she asked, "Want some?" in a cheeky voice.

Michael chuckled. "Sure I do. I want more than some." He leaned closer just as the guy on her right handed his credit card to the waitress. "I'll sit right here," Michael pointed. "You're done, right, Jack?"

"Yep," the man answered. "Have at it." He stepped off the stool as Michael slipped on.

Dixie slid the glass toward him. "I heard you have a girlfriend," she said.

He took the glass and then a long draw on the straw. "Yep, that's what everyone says."

Something in his words and the tone of his voice made her wonder. *Is he confirming his relationship or not?*

He took one more sip, a satisfying gurgle emitting from the bottom of the glass.

She looked him over carefully. "So am I driving with you or do I meet you at the construction site?"

"Drive with me. We can talk on the way."

Dixie pulled out her wallet and left a bill on the counter. "Keep the change," she called out to the waitress.

"See you next time," the woman replied.

"Not likely," Dixie muttered.

But she had to admit at least to herself, *I like this place. It has a good vibe.*

9

MARLA'S PLACE

She belted herself in as Michael backed his truck out of the parking space. "Is this your first chance to take in the scenery without driving?" he asked.

"I didn't come up here for the scenery," she mumbled, looking out her window anyway.

"I didn't either, but eventually it got to me." He smiled over at her.

"I'm not easily persuaded," she added. "In case you think otherwise. Skye informed me about your girlfriend."

"You mean Marla Osbourne?"

"Skye wanted to rush in and save me from myself. And save my reputation..." Dixie felt her hand clench. *I am now even more certain that I need to be a city cop. Small towns make me sick. Who I date is no one's business.*

Michael pointed over her shoulder. "There's a deer."

She couldn't help herself; she looked quickly. "Check him out. Antlers and everything. Looks like he's posing for a Christmas card."

"Arlo told me you were around for the setting up. I can't

help but wonder why a tourist would care so much and take her time to get to know the locals by volunteering."

Have I blown my cover? Dixie wondered.

"Just saying thank you to Meadow. She offered me a place to stay for free."

She watched his strong hand grip the wheel as he took a curve in the road, and then she looked straight ahead.

"You ever ride a motorcycle? You drive like someone who has."

"As a matter of fact I had a bike years ago. Then I dumped it and hurt my knee pretty bad. Sold it and bought a truck. All of that before Lily Rock."

She nodded, admiring how he paid attention to the road. She felt safe. Not a usual feeling for her, unless she was behind the wheel.

When the road straightened he looked at her again out of the corner of his eye. "You ask a lot of questions for an insurance person."

You're not gonna catch me, buddy. I got moves you can't even imagine. She began to spin her backstory, relishing every detail.

"Oh, you gotta know about vehicles in my line of work. Motorcycles cause a lot of accidents. They are the bread and butter of the industry. All of you who crash and burn become my problem, until I can prove that you are negligent."

"You don't have to pay out if that happens?"

"That's right. You might want to slow down. You're over the speed limit." She nodded toward the dial and added, "Just sayin'."

He chuckled.

Not exactly the response she'd intended. *Be afraid, you crazy overconfident man.*

He made a quick right, then a left down a gravel path.

The truck bumped along the uneven road. Gravel crunched as he headed toward the woods.

"That's the town namesake, right? Lily Rock." She pointed to where the rock formation was visible through the trees.

"That's it."

"More like an overgrown boulder."

"You don't have to be big to make a difference," he commented, giving her another sly glance.

She snorted.

"This is Marla's place. She's my employer." He pulled the truck closer to a double-wide trailer. It looked bigger than the house Dixie grew up in, with a porch in front and a large picture window. Her eyes drifted to the back of the lot where she could see signs of construction.

"You poured the slab already?"

He nodded. "It took nearly a year to get the permits. I had to cozy up to the Old Rockers and then become indispensable by putting up lights for the holidays and just making myself a general handyman. Eventually I moved up here permanently.

"The people got to know me better. Then I was hired for another project by Arlo and Doc. That's the brew pub. For whatever reason, the rest of the Old Rockers decided to trust me. The permits were signed soon after. Took months."

She heard the pride in his voice. Once he turned off the engine she opened her door. He came around the tailgate to stand next to her as she looked toward Lily Rock.

He pointed. "As you can tell, the back of the house will face Lily Rock and the woods. There will be a hot tub over there and a place for a garden." She followed his gaze.

"Looks like another cabin back there."

"That's my place. I built a small caretaker's unit to stay in while I supervise the project." He scratched the back of his neck. "I like it here. Still kind of surprises me though."

"Swallowed the Lily Rock Kool-Aid," she commented dryly. "Good luck with that."

"Maybe a bit sweet at times." He nodded. "Come with me. I want to introduce you to Marla. She's been waiting. I told her about you last night."

He told her about me. Are they laughing at me, thinking I was dazzled by his handsome good looks? Some couples do that, letting the other one flirt to spark up their love life.

She walked toward the trailer. The door opened and a tall thin woman stepped onto the porch, waving her hand. Her blond hair hung around her shoulders in soft waves. Even from a distance Dixie could see she'd been put together expensively. Leather boots, tight-fitting high-end jeans. *Just dressing her costs more than a month of my salary.*

A fitted wool sweater showed her curves and the big sapphire ring on her finger doubled down on Dixie's first impression.

"Hello there, you must be Dixie," Marla said in a low sultry voice.

She resisted the urge to say, "What's it to ya?" She cleared her throat before answering, "Yep, that's me, Dixie Jones, and you are Marla. Quite the place you have here."

Marla looked back over her shoulder. "Oh, you mean the trailer. It's only temporary. Michael's building me a fabulous house that will be ready by the end of next year." She stepped closer to him, holding his arm with both hands. "Won't it, sweetie? You promised."

He shrugged.

Dixie watched Marla closely. *She's certainly sure of herself and of him. An odd pair. I would have thought he'd go for a more sensitive type. Someone unaware of her own allure. This lady is clever and high maintenance and...*

Now that she stood directly in front of Marla, Dixie took

the opportunity to look more closely into the woman's face. *Something about her eyes, as if she's waiting to be judged. She's trying to be light-hearted but she's afraid of something. I wonder what...*

The sound of an alert came from Michael's cell phone, interrupting her assessment.

"An emergency?" Dixie asked. Michael stared at his screen.

"Yes, it is!" He shoved the phone back in his pocket. "Dixie, get into the truck. I've gotta get back to town."

"Should I come along?" Marla sounded frantic.

"You stay here. I can handle this." He grabbed Dixie by the arm, pulling her along. "It's a fire. I'm a volunteer. Got my gear in the back of the truck. Come on. This is your lucky day. You'll get to see Lily Rock in action."

10

SHE'S DOWN

Sirens wailed, filling the air with squawks and wails. Michael parked his truck along the side of the road. Dixie watched the night sky light up with flying embers overhead. She strained to see across the parking lot as the combination of dusk settling in and smoke made visibility difficult. Most of Lola's had already been engulfed in fire, the roof collapsing.

She felt a shiver up her spine.

Michael, jumping from the driver's seat, rummaged in the back of the truck. She slammed her door, walking toward the tailgate. He stood in the bed holding a worn jacket in the air.

He shoved one arm then the other into the jacket sleeves. Zipped closed, she saw his name on the front along with the letters: Lily Rock Volunteer First Responder.

"You've done this before?" she asked.

"More than a couple of times. We get lots of fires up here, but I suppose you already know that." He hopped to the ground in one easy move.

She pointed to a rope tied to the back of the toolbox. "You'll need that."

"Got it." He looked up. "Thanks, and sorry about all of this. Not the evening I'd planned."

"Never mind all that. Do you need any help?" She didn't want to admit that she had a lot of experience with burning buildings, especially when a dead body got in the mix. Her small town in Ohio had its share of arsonists.

"I bet you could help, you know, bring your insurance perspective to the situation." His voice sounded serious.

"Oh, right." She nodded.

He handed her the rope. Then he pulled out a wrinkled bandana from the jacket pocket. Tying it at the back of his neck, he slipped the fabric over his nose and mouth. "Going in. You stay out of trouble." Rope around his arm, he sprinted away.

She watched as he headed straight toward the blaze. *I could help out, but I might blow my cover.* She felt alert and uncomfortable. *I don't like doing nothing. It's not me.*

She felt her gut twist. The thought of Lily Rock burning to the ground made her angry. *They may be goofy, but they don't deserve this.* She watched as flames snaked over the dry earth, seeking grass and bushes for more fuel.

Wrapping her coat closer to her body, she began to walk toward the blaze. *Ping* went her cell phone. A text from the captain.

Just heard about fire. Stay out of the way. That's an order.

Too late, Caps. She shoved the cell in her back pocket. "He's not the boss of me," she said aloud. The blatant lie spoken to no one in particular made her smile. She picked up her pace, making her way toward a group of people hovering in the parking lot near the blaze.

They all watched as the shrubs surrounding Lola's burned, flames reaching higher. One volunteer climbed the side of the building, disappearing through an open window.

Dixie glanced upward. Two sequoias wore fiery hats, blazing in the night sky. The fire had inched its way up the tall trunks, searching for fuel in the air above. She heard the howl of the wind moving through the branches.

A crack made her jump. She looked above and saw a large sequoia branch making a fiery descent toward the ground.

"Move!" someone called.

Dixie lunged backward just in time. The branch bounced along the dirt, sending sparks into the air. It rolled to a stop a few feet away. She inhaled smoke, her chest heaving. After a quick cough she called out, "Need any help?"

A man turned. It was Arlo. "Come on over. Maybe you can lend a hand."

She kicked debris out of the path, watching where she stepped. "I can't believe the sequoias are burning," came a familiar voice.

Reaching out her hand, she gave the woman's shoulder a squeeze. Meadow's face, a mask of grief, stared at the charred branches. "We should have done something sooner. Taken the place in hand before all of this happened."

Dixie nodded and then glanced at Arlo. Half of his face covered in soot, his head hanging down. "We tried to talk to them," Arlo said, his voice filled with regret. "No one would listen. The townspeople are stubborn that way."

A voice shouted from the direction of Lola's. "Has anyone seen old man Maguire?"

Arlo and Meadow looked at each other and then at Dixie. She shrugged. "I wouldn't be able to recognize him. We've never met."

Arlo shouted back, "The cops from Riverside aren't here yet. I wish they'd move faster. We may have an arsonist in Lily Rock." He looked around frantically, panic in his voice.

She shook her head, willing herself to stay calm and

neutral. "Has anyone been able to get inside Lola's to look for Maguire?" She tried to give them a suggestion without sounding as if she knew what to do.

"We got a quick glimpse," Arlo said. "Got a couple people out. They were sitting in a booth, too stunned to evacuate."

"Good job," Dixie said in an uncharacteristic attempt at being encouraging. She'd kept out of the building, but not because she didn't want to run in there. Not taking action made her hands shake. *Stay put. Let them do the work. Don't take charge unless you have to.*

"But we didn't find Maguire," Meadow said. "He's one of us. An Old Rocker."

"A good guy, as good as they come," Arlo added.

Dixie looked away, not certain that she had one more neutral remark left. She wanted to get closer, to see what she could find and maybe help rescue people stuck in the building. Her legs tingled, begging to run and get involved.

Meadow was right. Not just about the sequoias. A rundown bar. An old man inside. A bunch of bikers. And no one thought to remove the debris off the property, to cut down the weeds. They were probably waiting for the snow to take care of things; that wait cost them. Sometimes you gotta take action.

Here I am standing on the sidelines watching. Judging Lily Rock residents for not looking ahead for potential danger. And then I just stand here knowing I could help. Her jaw tightened, hands began to tremble.

That's enough! No cover or professional detachment is worth me risking my own integrity.

As soon as she realized her next step, her hands stopped shaking and her legs stopped tingling. She sprinted toward Lola's.

"What are you doing?" Arlo called after her.

She didn't turn around to answer. Instead she picked up

the pace so as not to be detained. Heading directly toward the blaze, she felt the heat of the fire on her face. Holding her hand over her mouth, she stepped under the doorframe into the main room. She stopped to look around.

Her eyes fell on a man standing in the middle of the room. It was Michael. His face and head covered in soot, his gloved hands hung by his side. She gave him a nod. He nodded back.

He lowered his mouth covering, then pointed. "That melted goo over there? Plastic seat coverings from the booths. The rest is just rubble of what used to be."

"Meadow is worried about Maguire," she told him.

Michael pointed to a room beyond the bar. "I'm heading back there to look for him."

Then a voice called out, "We got Maguire. In the storeroom!"

Michael pulled up his bandanna, running in the direction of the voice. He disappeared through the doorway. She rushed to catch up, but a few steps forward, she stumbled. A loose board gave way under her foot. Her ankle twisted, accompanied by a sharp pain. Losing her balance, she lunged forward. Her hands hit the floor first and her body followed, her leg twisted underneath. She cried out with pain.

With one foot trapped underneath the floorboards, she lifted herself into a seated position. She bent one knee and pulled the trapped leg. Biting her bottom lip against the pain, she kept trying, but it hurt too badly to keep pulling. "I'm down!" she yelled. Smoke filling her lungs. She coughed, gasping for air.

She heard him first, and then saw Michael coming around from behind the bar.

"Let me help," he said, bending over to check her foot.

She held her hand over her mouth, taking short breaths as the smoke filled her lungs. Then she felt his hands around her leg, tugging gently at first. Then with one quick wrench, her leg was free.

"Oh yeah," she groaned. "That's the way to do it. Hurts!"

"I know and I'm sorry. But I got your foot free. Let's see if we can get you on your feet."

She felt his hands under both armpits. In one swift motion he lifted her to a standing position. She struggled to get her balance, unable to put weight on her one leg.

"I might have broken my ankle." She tried putting her foot down again and cried, "That hurts!"

He steadied her, reaching around her body so that she could balance against him, keeping the weight off of her injured ankle. "Let's get you out of here."

Together they hobbled through the smoke-filled room toward what used to be the front entrance. "But what about Maguire?"

Michael shook his head. "They already found him. Nothin' we can do now. Let's focus on what can be fixed. Your ankle."

She clung to his side, using her good leg for balance. One step, then the next, they hobbled out of the building. Away from the active fire's reach, he lifted her into his arms. "The paramedics are over there. Hang on."

11

OUCH!

Her leg hung outside the bathtub, wrapped in a plastic trash bag, secured on her thigh by duct tape. "That will keep your wound dry," Meadow assured her earlier. "And here's a washcloth. Your face is caked with dirt." She'd left Dixie to her own devices after that, closing the bathroom door behind her.

Dixie shuddered. *I've only been in Lily Rock for a couple of days. Already I'm getting treated like a child. Wash your face. Keep your leg dry. Do this. Do that.* Then the memory of Michael Bellemare swinging her into his arms made her pause. *Maybe it's not that bad.*

She ducked her face toward the warm bubbles floating on the water. Moistening the cloth, she rubbed it over her skin. Ripples of grime washed away. *Bathing in my own filth. I'm a shower woman, not some kind of draw-me-a-bath-and-bring-on-the-bubbles kind of girl.*

Letting the cloth drop into the bath water, she removed the band from her hair and shook it loose, running fingers through the tangles. *And how am I supposed to get my hair washed to get this smoky smell out with one leg hanging over the side, trussed and wrapped in plastic?*

Oh, I know. Meadow will make me an appointment at the local salon to wash my hair. Then I can have my nails done and get a pedicure. Grrrrr. She shifted her body backward, feeling the water rise over her belly. Even though her leg dangled over the side of the tub, she had to admit the water felt good. She relaxed her back and groaned as the muscles in her thigh tightened, causing a sharp twinge in her ankle. She bit her bottom lip to push back the pain. A knock came at the door.

Meadow's voice trilled, "It's getting late, dear. Do you need help getting out of the tub?"

"No," Dixie shouted. She regretted her refusal as soon as her ankle protested with another throb of pain.

The doc's examination earlier had revealed a break, not a sprain. He'd wrapped a boot around her calf, securing it in place. "That will keep the swelling down," he'd told her. Then he'd given her a handful of painkillers. "Take one every four hours for the next two days."

After that things were a blur until she'd ended up in the bathtub. *How will I get out of this swill by myself?*

She sank her hands into the water, her fingers trying to find purchase against the slippery bottom of the tub. *That's not gonna work.* Twisting her body, she grabbed the side of the tub with both hands. With a heave she rolled her butt up and then over, using her good leg to balance until she could stand on one foot. Weaving from side to side she grabbed the sink for balance.

Like a whale. That's what I feel like. One big bunch of mammal, lame and useless, flopping around. Aware that the tile floor would be slippery, she made small steps toward the bath mat. Still clinging to the sink, she rested her sore foot on the mat but then pulled it back up immediately.

Dixie gasped, holding in her pain. *Shush. You don't want*

Meadow rushing in to towel you off, now do you? Your naked flesh is your own business. As if to contradict her own inner reasoning, Michael Bellemare's worried face came to mind. Dixie took a minute to relish the feeling from earlier, when he carried her in his arms.

"I'll wait out here until you're done with the doc," he'd said earlier.

"What about the fire?"

"Things are under control. All we have to do is sort through the rubble and keep an eye on any embers. Plus it's supposed to snow." He'd smiled at her then, a look of apology in his eyes. "I'm really sorry about all of this."

Dixie was seated next to him in the doc's waiting room, her leg thrust out in front of her body. She squirmed and winced. "Not your fault. I ran into the building."

He smiled. "What were you thinking?"

She didn't answer because she really didn't know for sure. *What was I thinking? It was instinct. I'm a cop, and I've been trained to run headlong into danger.* The faint sense of regret was instantly overpowered by a feeling she wasn't familiar with.

I wanted to help these people. Lily Rock, the town, has been pretty nice to me overall. Basically I've just lied to them and tried to get away with it. She shook her head, feeling disgusted with herself and not very professional. *Go away, teeny tiny feelings. Get the ankle fixed and get back to LA where you belong.*

A knock came to the bathroom door, bringing Dixie back to the present.

"I have a big bath towel for you," came Meadow's voice.

She glanced over as another pain shot up her leg. "Oh okay," she said loudly. "Come on in and give me a hand. But keep your eyes closed."

The doorknob turned.

* * *

By the time she'd dried off, Dixie wondered what she'd wear. Her clothes were filthy and smelled like smoke. Looking toward the dresser, she saw a mound of clothing neatly folded next to it. *I suppose those are for me.* She hopped over to grab the top item. Slipping the skirt over her body, the fabric fell down in ripples, covering her injured leg, sitting loosely at her waist. The top came next, an off-the-shoulder peasant blouse.

One glimpse into the mirror made her groan. *Am I going to a Renaissance Fair?*

Running her fingers through her wet curls, she stared at her reflection. *If the captain saw me in this getup, he'd think I'd been abducted and tortured and become a time traveler. Or at the very least forced into work as a barmaid.*

She scooted backward to sit on the bed. Putting one filthy trainer on her good foot, she gingerly tested the weight on the broken ankle. *Ouch. Why do I keep trying to put weight on this leg? It won't heal magically. I'll have crutches by tomorrow.* Then another thought made her groan. *I don't think I can safely drive yet. Stuck in Lily Rock.*

Opening the door, down the hall she went. Thumps and slides got her to the kitchen where she found Meadow stirring a large pot on the stove.

"Navy bean soup," she said, "and hunks of sourdough. Eat some and I'll get your next pain pill. Plus I have tea waiting to be brewed. A little mixture of mine that will help you relax and get a good night's sleep. Just herbs. Nothing fancy."

Dixie slid closer to the table. Two chairs had been pulled out, one with a pillow on the seat.

"Sit on that one. The other is for you to elevate your ankle.

Skye told me to keep administering fresh cold packs for the next twenty-four hours."

Dixie put her hands on the edge of the table. She sat down gingerly, her ankle throbbing.

Meadow brought a large mug of soup, setting it in front of Dixie. She slid a basket closer. Chunks of bread, piled inside, smelled faintly of fresh sourdough. "I have butter too," Meadow announced. She came back with a crock of butter and an ice bag.

Dixie watched as she placed the butter on the table and then turned to wrap the ice in a towel. Bending over, she grasped the back of Dixie's knee as she elevated the ankle to rest on the other chair. Then she placed the ice on top of the ankle.

"Thank you," she mumbled, her ankle becoming blissfully cold through the boot.

Lifting the mug to her lips, Dixie inhaled first. She didn't bother with the spoon. Taking a sip, she felt the warm liquid slide down her throat, leaving a slight aftertaste of honey and ham.

"You put ham in the soup?" she said, her teeth mashing into a delicious portion.

"Honey-baked," Meadow insisted. "This soup has curative powers. Everyone says so."

She took another sip, forgetting about the pain in her ankle.

With a spoon she dug for chunks of meat, giving her a chance to think. *This ankle may keep me in place for who knows how long. The captain will be furious.* Looking up, she froze. The doorknob of the back door turned.

Michael Bellemare stepped inside. She exhaled quickly with relief.

He looked at Dixie, then Meadow. "Seems like the patient is doing just fine."

"Come in, dear," Meadow offered. "Soup's on."

"Don't mind if I do." He closed the door behind him.

Observing Dixie's wrapped leg, he said, "Good you have ice on it."

Is everyone in Lily Rock a doctor now?

He moved closer to the table, eyes still on her ankle. Then he looked into her eyes. "So, Dixie Jones," he said, a bit formally, "you rushed into that burning bar as if you'd done it before. Are you sure you want to keep pretending to be an insurance adjuster?" His eyes flashed, daring her to disagree.

God, he's handsome. But I'm not giving up my cover. Not even for him.

"Part of my insurance training," she glibly replied. "I mostly sit behind a desk, but I've also inspected buildings."

"If you say so." He winked and then walked around to pull out a chair. Meadow had already placed a full mug of soup on the table.

She shoved the bread basket toward him. "Just eat, dear, and stop asking nosy questions. Our Dixie will tell you when she's ready."

Our Dixie...

A slight smile came to her lips. To her surprise tears formed in her eyes. She ducked her head to hide her face, feeling oddly emotional. *She called me "our Dixie." It got to me.* Head still bent, she dabbed at her eyes with the napkin.

Must be the drugs. Or the soup.

12

SMART, FEISTY, AND SLIGHTLY DISHEVELED

With a dab here and there, she lifted her eyes. Michael stared right at her, a slight smile on his lips.

If only I could tell him the truth. He's so smart and alert. The kind of guy who would make a great partner, someone I could rely on. She remembered how he'd reacted when she broke her ankle. How he took charge right away, without fussing or making her feel stupid.

She glared at him across the table. "Eat your soup and stop staring at me." *One more chunk of bread.* She stuffed it into her mouth and chewed.

After swallowing she looked back at Michael. He leaned over the table with his arms crossed in front of him. She cleared her throat.

"So I was wondering. What happened to that Maguire character? He must have a first name. You don't actually call him old man Maguire to his face." She tried to look interested but not too keen.

"We just called him old man Maguire," Meadow said, her voice growing quiet. "I think his first name was Alfred. No one ever mentioned that. He didn't like the name but didn't seem to mind that we called him old man at all."

Michael nodded. "It was hard to ruffle him. He was unflappable."

Dixie noticed the use of the past tense. "So Alfred Maguire..."

"He's gone," Meadow sighed.

"The first responders thought it was smoke inhalation," Michael added. "They took him away. I don't know exactly where."

"Autopsy," Dixie said, before she could stop herself. Scrambling to cover herself she added, "I only know that because of other insurance cases. I've read reports. That's what they do when a body is found in a fire."

Despite the circumstances, Michael smirked.

Unable to leave it alone, Dixie continued, "So where does Lily Rock take cases like this, when further investigation is required?"

"Riverside County Police," Meadow answered immediately. "We don't get a lot of their attention, so it may take a while before they issue a report. Some of the newer residents think we need a cop up here on the hill full-time. So far Riverside can't spare anyone. The police force is already stretched too thin." She adjusted the napkin over the bread basket.

This may be a sensitive topic for Meadow. She seems a bit nervous, fiddling with that napkin.

Meadow kept explaining, "The Old Rockers aren't in any hurry for police up here. We handle everything in our own way."

Dixie clamped her lips shut, realizing she wanted to disagree with Meadow. *So the tension is between those who want a local cop in Lily Rock and those who think it's unnecessary.*

She took the last sip of soup. *I better call the captain. He'll be wondering what I've been up to. Can't wait to hear him yell when I tell him about my injured ankle.*

She looked down at the bag of ice, which now dripped onto the kitchen tile. Her toes felt cold and slightly numb.

Meadow pushed her chair back. "I'll get you more ice. I also have homemade sugar cookies for dessert." She turned to Michael. "Your favorite, the ones with the thick frosting and decoration."

He leaned back in his chair, folding his arms across his chest.

Dixie wiggled her toes and winced.

He stared at her and then shook his head. "It's gonna hurt for a few days. Have you tried to walk?"

"Got in here, didn't I?"

"She took a bath," commented Meadow, placing a plate of cookies on the table. She removed the bag of melted ice from Dixie's ankle, replacing it with a bag of frozen peas. "That should work for now," she explained.

"You took a bath with that?" He pointed to her leg.

"I have a high pain threshold," Dixie commented, biting into a cookie. The taste of butter and lemon filled her mouth; the sweetness brought a smile to her lips. *How can one bite taste like Christmas...*

"Man, these are excellent cookies!" she announced.

Meadow's smile lit up her face. "Why thank you, dear. Sage says my Christmas cookies are her favorite. She'll be home tomorrow for the tree lighting." Then her smile faded. "But it's probably cancelled. The decorations have all been destroyed by the heat and flames."

"Maybe not," Michael said. "We can clean up and light a small tree instead."

Meadow's voice dropped. "What about the sequoias? They're probably all dead. What will we ever do?"

Dixie felt her heart twist. *Those big ol' trees must feel like people to her.*

"Hire a tree expert," Dixie said. "I bet you can save the sequoias. Ones up north have survived worse than a small timber fire. I've heard they store up their energy in the enormous trunks and get new roots and grow more branches or something."

When Meadow and Michael didn't respond, she just kept talking. "I mean, I don't know exactly how the trees do it, but I bet an arborist would have good suggestions. You must have one somewhere in Lily Rock. They hang out in log cabins and look like crazy people. You know the type."

Meadow chuckled. Michael outright guffawed. "You got that right. You're so observant, even after only being here a couple of days. We have arborists lined up to give us advice about those sequoias. The problem won't be finding an expert but picking the right one."

"The most sane one, you mean." Dixie reached for another cookie and held it up. A reindeer, frosted white with snowflake sparkles. She bit off the head.

Michael stood to his feet. "So why don't you finish up here. And then I'll get you back into bed."

She ducked her chin and kept munching. He stood over her, grinning as if he enjoyed making her uncomfortable.

Once she'd finished, he bent closer and swept her into his arms.

"Hero to the rescue," remarked Meadow with a laugh.

Dixie wrapped an arm around his neck. Unlike earlier that evening, he smelled like soap and aftershave. *I'm not the only one who cleaned up.*

He carried her down the hall, kicking the door open. He settled her on the bed. "Lie down," he told her in a firm voice.

She fell back. "You certainly have a way with the women." She smirked at him.

"Lift your head," he commanded. When she complied he slid a pillow underneath. "Now scoot back," he insisted.

She did so without a complaint.

He left the room and then returned with pillows from the sofa. "I'm going to put your foot up on these to keep it elevated. I hope you can get comfortable that way." He pushed aside the covers. "I know this will hurt, but just for a minute." He gently raised her leg.

She sat up a bit watching him, strangely detached from her pain. She didn't want to make a fuss; he was trying so hard. When the foot was propped, she leaned back against the pillows, willing the pain to subside.

"Sleep tight," he told her, pulling a coverlet to her chin.

Her eyes slid closed. She had lost all the energy it took to keep them open. "You realize I'm wearing a skirt and top right now?" Her voice sounded tired to her own ears.

"Just call them pajamas. No one knows but us."

She felt him adjust the blanket again.

"Did you just tuck me in?"

"I did. I also have one more question. You can keep your eyes closed. Meadow is busy, so now's the time."

Dixie tried to open her eyes to no avail. She felt woozy. "Do you want to make out or something? I'm lame and helpless and must be quite a sight in this skirt and my hair all a mess. Is that how you like your women?"

"That's not what I'm talking about. If you must know I like my women smart and feisty and yes, slightly disheveled. I'd also like you to tell me the truth. What's your real name and how did you end up in Lily Rock?"

Dixie felt a fog settle over her brain. She could hear him

talking but could not distinguish the words. Smiling slightly her lips went slack; her ankle had finally stopped aching.

67

13

THUMP AND HOIST

Dixie groaned as a sharp pain shot up her leg. It felt as if someone had reattached her ankle with hot glue.

What if I'd broken my back or my neck. I'm just a weenie. It was her habit to make herself feel better by remembering how bad it could have been. She opened one eye, then the other. She stared at the ceiling and then turned her head toward the bedside table.

Her cell phone lay upside down on a doily. *Maybe Michael left it there last night.* A smile crept to her lips, right before she felt a sense of dread. *Did I tell him my name? I was pretty fuzzy and tired. Maybe I did and I don't remember.* She reached for her cell phone, holding it in the air to check her messages.

Five missed calls from the captain. She pushed redial and held the phone up to her ear.

She used her happiest sounding voice. "Happy Christmas Eve day. If that's a thing. Any plans for this evening? Going to church?" She held the phone away from her ear as he ranted a reply.

Convinced that the storm had passed, she brought the

phone back to her ear. "I broke my ankle. That's why I didn't call."

"You what?"

"That's right. Ran into a burning building and fell through the floor, foot first." She closed her eyes, once again aware of the throbbing pain. "I need to take another pill, but I have to get breakfast first."

"So you're still in Lily Rock?"

"Yes, sir. On the job."

"Did you find out who is sending those anonymous emails? I wish our tech guys could give me more information. But the department isn't taking new cases until after Christmas, and ours sits at the bottom of the pile when they come back."

"That reminds me," Dixie said. "I wanted to tell you that I've felt a tension between the people who want a cop in Lily Rock and those who don't. I'm wondering if that's at the heart of those emails being anonymous..."

"Could be," the captain sounded thoughtful. "Good catch, Dixie," he added.

She felt his humor return. She shifted her voice to chatty. "So it's a good thing I'm out of your hair, recuperating on delicious soup and eating sumptuous Christmas cookies for dessert."

"Don't forget. You're fraternizing with potential criminals. I've warned you about the dangers of undercover work and getting too close."

Yeah, real bad guys in Lily Rock. There's the woman who lets people stay with her if they can't find a place. And the doc and his girlfriend who spend their time setting up the Christmas light festival. Not to forget the hunky architect, who by the way lifted me into his arms more than once yesterday.

"Yes, sir. I won't forget."

"When are you coming back?" he finally asked, using a voice that he reserved for children and the mentally disadvantaged.

"I don't know, Caps. Sage is coming home from school and we have yet to find the missing baby Jesus. Plus old man Maguire passed away in the fire and the Old Rockers are pretty upset by that. Oh, and don't forget Meadow. She's calling in a local arborist to consult about the sequoias." Instead of pausing for his response, Dixie kept talking.

"Those trees are a big priority in Lily Rock. I'll try to work a ride back to Los Angeles into the conversation today, but I doubt anything will be arranged until some of those other issues are resolved." She finally paused to take a quick breath and jumped back in before he got a word in edgewise. "Did I mention I broke my ankle?"

"Is there a 'yes, sir, Captain' in any of that nonsense?"

"Yes, sir."

"I think your rush into the burning building may have been a mistake. You could have lost your cover by getting too involved. Remember that as a warning, recruit."

"Yes, sir." It was all she could do to hold the phone, waiting for him to say goodbye first.

Only then was she willing to admit to herself that by running into that burning building, she may have upended her undercover assignment. *I should have let them handle their own problems. Impulsive and unprofessional.*

Her fingers wrapped into a fist as she thumped the mattress. Her inner voice spoke up. *On one hand, I made a huge mistake getting close to these people, but on the other hand? I want to smell pine trees and to see Christmas and to have friends.* As she considered her dilemma she heard someone call from the hallway.

"Are you awake, dear?" came Meadow's soft voice.

And I want more soup and a pain pill right now!

She brushed the back of her hand over her eyes, wiping away tears of pain and frustration. "I'm awake. Come on in."

Meadow opened the door, a folded pile of laundry in one arm.

Dixie stood by the side of the bed. Leaning against the mattress, she'd wrapped a sheet around her body after taking off the clothes lent to her. "Thanks for the skirt." She handed it to Meadow with relief, then pointed to the familiar stack of clothes Meadow held in her arm. "And thanks for doing my laundry. Really you shouldn't have."

"I love the smell of clean clothes," Meadow replied. "Plus I had to get yours in and out before Sage gets home later today. She'll have loads and loads of laundry from school."

"How old is your daughter?" Dixie asked, not because she cared but because it was the polite thing to do.

"Finishing an advanced degree in school administration," Meadow said, her voice filled with pride. "I hope she'll take on the Lily Rock Music Academy very soon. The Old Rockers think she'd be a perfect fit for principal."

"Does Lily Rock usually hire like that, from within the community? I've heard that's common for small towns."

"I don't know about other small towns," Meadow answered, "but Lily Rock keeps things in the family, so to speak. We hire from within first. But Sage will be qualified," she added, giving Dixie a firm nod. "She'll have nothing to feel ashamed of."

"I'd better get dressed," Dixie said. "And I need a ride to town, if that's possible."

"You have to check in with the doctor." Meadow nodded. "I think Michael said he'd drive by and pick you up."

Once she'd dressed and eaten breakfast, she felt a lot better. The pain pill took the edge off of her discomfort. This time she didn't jump when the doorknob turned. Michael came through the door, carrying a pair of crutches.

He smiled, holding them out for her to inspect.

She reached over to grab them, heaving herself up from the chair. Thumping them both down ahead of herself, she practiced walking and hoisted her body to catch up. A few more tries and she got the hang of it, making her way around the kitchen table. Michael stood by and watched.

Dixie's head buzzed. She closed her eyes, willing the dizziness to stop. She felt woozy now that she was exerting some effort. "Lead the way," she told him with more confidence than she felt.

"You're pretty good with those." He gestured to the crutches.

"I've had my share of injuries," she mumbled.

"I thought you mostly sat behind a desk. Insurance must be a lot more strenuous than I ever realized." He smirked at her. She winced with pain.

He reached out to take her elbow. "I'd like to drive past Lola's and assess the fire damage before going to Doc's. Want to come along?"

"So long as I get to come with you," she retorted. "I want to see what's left of Lola's and where I fell through the floor."

Thump, hoist. Thump, hoist. She headed toward the back door.

"I'll get you a jacket," he offered.

She nodded. Balancing her body with the crutches took all of her concentration.

14

THE SEARCH CONTINUES

Standing inside the burned-out Lola's, Dixie assessed the situation. *The fire appears to be out. Good job, volunteers.* Her eyes took in puffs of smoke lifting up next to where the bar once stood. But as far as she could tell, there were no more burning embers.

She sniffed. Underneath the obvious smell of burned wood, she felt a crispness to the air. She wrapped her jacket closer to her body, a shiver sprinkling down her spine.

"You from snow country?" Michael stood next to her, looking outward from where a wall once stood. His face looked solemn.

"Born and raised in Southern California. I thought I wanted to get away from it all and live in a small town. You know, a place with snow and log fires. I mostly know snow from skiing on vacations." She stared down at her boot. "Or at least I used to."

"You'll heal really fast. Not to worry. The doc is a ladies' man, but don't let that fool ya. He sets a broken bone like a pro." Michael encouraged her with a smile. "Sure you don't want to sit down on a bench?" He pointed across the way. The bench, made of stone, looked very tempting. *If I sit down I may not want to get back up.*

She shrugged and changed the subject. "There's no concrete slab." She pointed to the floor where her leg had gotten caught; the wood exposed the dirt.

"They didn't require permits back in the day. Lots of people built right on the dirt."

Dixie cocked her head to the side. A familiar voice came from a few feet away. "We could put a small tree with battery-powered lights right there. I can make a basket for the creche." Meadow pointed to a clearing in the woods. Arlo stood by her side.

"That would work. Finding a small tree will be no problem this time of year. I'd like to give Paws and Pines another look. Maybe the baby Jesus will show up in one of their storage units behind the kennel." Arlo patted Meadow's back.

"Doc said he already checked. But we can look again. Hello, dear." Meadow caught sight of Dixie. She and Arlo walked closer. "We were just discussing our Christmas Eve tree lighting ceremony. It's still on for tonight."

Feeling somewhat surprised, Dixie shook her head. "I thought for sure you'd cancel the festivities, what with the fire and all."

"We're gonna scale it down," Arlo admitted. He looked into the grove where just a day ago they'd set up reindeer, a Santa, and the holy family. Dixie followed his gaze. She saw lumps of plastic where the menorah and wise men had melted into the dirt.

"It sure is a mess," she said.

"We can get new things for next year. They'll be on sale right after the holidays. I have some petty cash from the Old

Rocker fund." To her credit, Meadow only sounded a little bit forced.

Dixie cleared her throat. "Speaking of Old Rockers, what about old man Maguire? Have they finished with the body?"

Michael looked at Dixie, his eyebrow raised.

Then Meadow spoke. "He's been taken to Come Rest Awhile Mortuary. We can have a service and wake in January."

"What about his biker friends? Do they know that he's... gone?" Arlo asked.

"I know Rich. I'll text him and he can inform everyone else." Michael pulled out his cell.

Dixie's face scrunched. "I still want to know how the fire started."

Arlo looked at the dirt. Michael shrugged. Meadow finally answered.

"The damage is done. We rarely call in outside experts. We take care of our own business."

"I am almost certain the fire wasn't caused deliberately by the bikers. They're a good group. I've known them for ages," Arlo said.

"Mostly noisy and smelly. But still friends of Lily Rock," added Meadow.

Dixie felt frustrated. Reports and solid evidence were the only way to bring closure to a situation like this. She wasn't convinced. "So you don't think the bikers may have started a fire, even by mistake?"

Michael butted in, "Sometimes a bike can spark a fire, but it's so cold. I don't imagine that happened."

Her stomach twisted with impatience. She leaned into her crutches to keep from losing her temper. Arlo spoke up next, saving her from overreacting.

"Probably an electrical issue. Old man Maguire rewired

Lola's himself a few years ago and he was, let's say, kind of a make-do guy."

Dixie's head swiveled back and forth from Michael to Arlo to Meadow. She clamped her mouth closed. *I'm here to gather information, not to solve a potential homicide by unintentional arson. They obviously think they can handle everything themselves. But I'm wondering if one of them may be our anonymous emailer.*

And that, ladies and gentlemen, is the problem with a town that used to be small but has grown over the years. The old ways stop working. Crime often thrives in a live and let live environment. Her mind continued to put pieces together, making sense of their obvious reluctance to look for the actual cause of the fire.

Instead of asking for help, the Old Rockers come to their own conclusions and I bet they administer their own justice. Meadow probably revokes a library card from the real baddies. She sighed. *Deliver me from amateur sleuths and volunteers.*

Dixie looked at the three of them, deep in conversation about how big the Christmas tree should be, acting oblivious to any other concerns. *Must be nice to be them.* A tingle of envy rose like a fly buzzing around her head. She blinked to make it stop.

She had arrived under false pretenses. And they'd been so kind. She had to admit, she'd changed her mind about Lily Rock in just the past couple of days. She felt like she wanted to be more like them, not so much an outsider.

"You were saying?" prompted Michael. He had stopped talking to Meadow and Arlo, directing his dark gaze toward her. She decided to change the subject.

"I may want to adopt a dog someday. How about I tag along with you to—what did you call it? Paws and Pines?"

"That's our local animal shelter, run by Doc. We have lots

of dogs and cats. A few rabbits. And three horses that were put out to pasture." Meadow smiled. "Do you ride?"

Dixie stared at her boot. "Not at the present time." She cleared her throat. "Doc owns the place?"

Michael gave her a side-eye. "And that's important because?"

With the crutches firmly under her armpits, she dragged her shoe in the dirt. "I'm just interested and want to help," she said blandly. Hiding her eyes from Michael felt like the right thing to do. *He's on to me.*

"Let's go," Arlo said immediately. "Afterward I want to show Dixie the plans for the new brew pub." He looked at her with a smile. "Michael finished the design and it's a doozie. Ol' Lily Rock is coming up in the world."

Michael cupped Dixie's elbow in his hand, ignoring Arlo's praise. "I'm driving with Dixie. Meet you at Paws and Pines." He dropped his hand, watching as she placed the crutches forward, hoisting her body to catch up.

They made slow progress back to the truck as Michael kept talking. "Marla didn't get a chance to tell you what was on her mind the other day. She still wants to talk. Maybe you could take some time after we visit Paws and Pines, or even better...I'll convince her to come to the tree lighting. She can chat with you then."

"Sounds good," Dixie said without argument. But in her head she wondered, *Why is he trying so hard to get us together?*

15

I'M A COP

A wooden sign with Paws and Pines Animal Shelter etched on the surface pointed the way. Michael turned off the engine and hopped out of the truck. He arrived on her side to open the door. "Here you go." He offered his hand, grasping her elbow.

After some hopping and adjusting, Dixie landed with her one foot on the ground and the other bent at the knee, holding onto both of his hands. "I still can't put any weight on it," she admitted.

"After Christmas we can send you down the hill to have a look by an orthopedist." He reached to grab the crutches from the back seat.

Growing more accustomed to the rhythm of walking with crutches, Dixie kept up with Michael as they headed toward the entrance. She caught sight of an old Quonset hut standing in the midst of the trees. *I wonder how long that's been here. It's about to fall over from the looks of it.* She came closer and saw that the front door stood ajar.

As they made their way to the front of the shelter, Dixie stopped and tilted her head to the side. After a moment she said, "I expected to hear a lot of barking. This is a very quiet shelter."

When they reached the entrance, Michael held the door open. "Now that you mention it, I rarely hear any noise when I come by." Dixie swung her way inside as he followed, the door closing behind him.

A few feet into the hut they stopped in front of a desk that separated the entrance area from a door that was closed. Michael rang the bell on the counter. A familiar young man appeared from behind the door, holding a roll of plastic bags.

"Just picking up poop," he explained. "How can I help you?"

"I know you!" Dixie exclaimed. "You handed out keys at the rental place."

He placed the roll of bags on the counter. "I don't remember you, but then again, there were a lot of people that day."

She sniffed, smelling a stronger scent wafting off of his jacket. *I wonder if a lot of the Lily Rock crowd keeps sane by smoking weed and drinking. It may be prejudice on my part, but the boredom must get to them, a small town with very little else to do.*

"Do you work here too?" Dixie asked the young man.

"I work wherever I can, but mostly at the garage."

She nodded. "I remember you mentioning the garage. And that you gave my cabin to someone else."

"Right," he said without any visible remorse. "First come, first served."

"Did you hear about the fire?" Michael asked.

The young man ran his fingers through his hair. "Oh yeah. I got there too late to help. Doc called me this morning to help out here."

Dixie wondered, *Would he be the kind of kid to toss a*

cigarette butt into the dirt and walk away, not knowing he could start a fire? Her jaw tightened. "Where were you yesterday afternoon around four o'clock?"

Michael stepped back, giving her the now familiar side-eye. The kid spoke right up. "I was picking up keys from people heading back down the hill. I have witnesses," he retorted.

"What's your name?" Dixie demanded.

"Brad. Brad May."

"Are you related to Doc May?"

"He's my uncle."

Another side-eye from Michael made Dixie inhale deeply. *He obviously thinks I'm overstepping my role as Lily Rock tourist with all of these questions. I want to get to the bottom of this fire business and Brad May is a suspect. A pot smoker. He's everywhere. I bet people think he's a May and untouchable. Plus he's up to something. He acts...nervous.*

Michael spoke up. "So, Brad, we're looking for the Christmas decorations stored here last year."

"I already checked when Meadow called a couple of days ago. No baby Jesus here." The kid folded his arms across his chest, looking defensive, at least to Dixie, who thought everyone was guilty until proven innocent.

Michael lowered his voice. "I'm not accusing you of anything." He glanced at Dixie as if to say, *Unlike some people.* "But I'd like to have a look in the shed out back, just to make sure stuff didn't get shoved into a corner and missed."

Brad reached under the counter and came up with a key. "Sure, go ahead." He slid the key across the counter to Michael's outstretched hand. On the way out, Dixie heard a howl coming from behind the closed door. *Okay, that's the first animal sound I've heard here other than human.*

She watched as Brad turned his back to open the door and

hurry away. A couple of scattered barks escaped as the door closed behind him. Dixie and Michael turned from the counter, heading toward the door.

Once outside, Dixie stopped to listen again. No dogs barking this time, but a low rumble sounded in the distance, and a sharp blast rang in the cold air. The increasing roar, more intense, finally manifested in a group of motorcycle riders coming from the main road. Two by two, they rolled over the dirt toward the shelter.

Dust flew into the air, making Dixie cough into her elbow. The first one to arrive shut off his engine and jumped off the seat. He came toward Michael, lifting his helmet, his face grim. "I heard about old man Maguire."

Michael nodded. "We lost him."

"Was it the fire?"

"Smoke inhalation, at least that's what they thought."

The man turned around and gestured to the rest of the gang by waving his hand in the air. One by one they parked their bikes and switched off their engines. They hopped off the bikes and stepped closer. Dixie took a deep breath, leaning into her crutches.

The bikers formed a semicircle behind the first man. Helmets held in hands, they all looked grim. Sad faces and downturned mouths met Dixie's inquisitive glare. The first man said, "Thanks for letting me know about old man Maguire and Lola's. We'd like to make a donation to the memorial fund."

Maybe that's the guy Michael said he knew. Her suspicion was immediately confirmed.

"That would be greatly appreciated, Rich. I'll send you details after the holidays." He looked over the entire group. "You're all welcome to the service too."

The leader nodded. He took a step backward, pulling on

his helmet. A voice from the crowd called out, "Still having Christmas? The light festival?"

Michael answered, "So far as we know. Scaled down, of course. But it's on for tonight."

The men stared at him and then one by one turned away. "We'll be there," one man finally called over his shoulder.

"Usual time?" asked another guy.

"Nine o'clock," Michael assured them.

As their leader got back on his bike, the rest filed behind him, putting helmets over their heads. Hopping on seats, several of the group started their engines. The rest did the same. A deafening noise like rolling thunder filled the air.

Dixie watched the gang speed away, dust flinging into the air. One motorcycle backfired, startling her. She shook her head. *A spark from a tail pipe could have caused the fire.* She watched the gang rumble out of sight before turning to Michael.

"Were they in town yesterday around four o'clock?"

He shrugged. "I don't know. I don't usually keep track." He looked at her intently. "You certainly are an inquisitive little thing, aren't you?"

"I am not a little thing."

He flushed. "You're right. Sorry about that. I know better than to talk about a woman's stature."

"There's been a fire, a death, and this place..." Dixie looked over her shoulder, "has an unsettling vibe."

"I think I know what you mean," he admitted, "but until you came I didn't realize the extent of what's happened right in front of me. You've made me look at Lily Rock differently, with your questions and nosy attitude."

Dixie felt a moment of pride. "I think you may have just complimented me and probably didn't intend to."

He nodded.

Since she'd arrived in Lily Rock, she'd made every attempt to look like a weekend tourist. But now she sensed she needed to come clean. She was going to follow her gut. *I need to take charge and move forward with an investigation. In some ways Lily Rock has no clue.* So she answered the question he had not directly asked.

"I'm a cop," she told him. "Actually the oldest recruit, back at the academy for further training. Lots of reasons for that, my previous experience included. I may or may not be assigned to a small town. It's up to my captain. He thought it would be a good thing to go undercover during my time off over the holidays. I'm here to assess the need for a Lily Rock police presence. But I have the feeling you already figured that out."

His lips drew a straight line. Finally he nodded. "I figured."

Using the energy from her confession, the relief she felt in speaking the truth, she added, "Now let's get to that shed. I'm kind of curious what's stored in there. And by the way? Dogs bark more incessantly at shelters. There's not enough noise around here."

"I figured you weren't who you said you were. Pretty interesting." He glanced at her crutches.

She nodded. "My gut tells me there's something odd going on here at Paws and Pines." She tucked her crutches under her arms. "So point me to that storage shed and bring the key."

"It's behind the kennels. I've got the key right here."

16

THE CLUE IN THE SHED

Michael used the key to open the lock to the shed as Dixie took a minute to lean on her crutches. One look inside made him groan. "This place has no rhyme or reason. No wonder the baby Jesus got lost."

Dog kennels, dog beds, old rabbit hutches were stacked to the ceiling—every corner was filled. "So Brad was the one to look in here for Jesus?" Dixie asked, sounding skeptical.

"And knowing Brad, I bet he didn't look that hard. Maybe that's why he acted so defensive. He probably opened the door, looked inside, and ran away."

Dixie nodded her agreement. Then she followed Michael inside the shed. He pulled down a chair from a stack in the corner and sat on it. Before she could say anything, he wiggled in the seat and stood up.

"Pretty sturdy. Why don't you sit there and give me directions. We'll start pulling this place apart."

She didn't bother to argue. Every muscle in her body ached. She sat with a thump, stretching her booted leg in front of her. "Thanks," she muttered, still not used to feeling grateful.

Michael disappeared behind a stack of boxes. She heard a thud. "You okay back there?"

He appeared holding a jumbled mass of red, white, and blue flags. "I've got summer flags and banners. We've been looking for those. Meadow will be pleased that she doesn't have to buy them for the next Memorial Day."

"She can be happy in May. This is December. Keep looking," grumbled Dixie.

Twenty minutes later, he stood back to assess his progress. "No baby Jesus, but at least all of the boxes are on this side and the extra cages and kennels are over there now." He nodded. "Let's look inside the boxes. If we don't find Jesus, we might have to assume he's left the building."

Dixie laughed. "Pretty funny. If I were religious I could make something of that."

Michael shrugged. "Okay then, let's tear these open and see what we can find."

"I'll help." She stood, but her good leg buckled as both crutches dropped to the floor. He lurched forward and grabbed her arm.

"A bit wobbly for a cop," he muttered, both hands at her shoulders, helping to keep her steady. He reached over to grab her crutches and hand them to her.

"The pain pills aren't helping," she admitted. Her eyes narrowed as she shrugged off his hands, dragging herself closer to the stack of boxes. "I'm getting a strong feeling about the contents of the boxes. This feels off." She tore open the top of the first box she came to. Then she reminded him, "We need to get a look at those dogs before we leave." Her voice softened. "Well lookie here..."

He came closer to peer inside. "Bottles and boxes," he said, "must be dozens of them." He ran his hand through the pile. "Basically two types."

She pulled up a bottle. "CBD supplement," she read. She dug back into the box for more.

This time she held a white container with labels on both sides. "Benadryl," she announced. With a twist of the lid, she used her fingernail to pull back the protective foil top. Bright pink pills spilled into her palm. "Unless I'm mistaken, what we have here are dozens of containers of medications, both antihistamines and CBD. It doesn't take an expert to know what's keeping the dogs quiet."

"They're being drugged?" Michael ran his hand through his hair, looking surprised. "That's stooping pretty low. If anyone knew about this, there would be trouble."

"That's what I'm thinking." Her jaw tightened. "And if the doc owns this place, I suspect he knows and may be behind all the quiet. Drug-induced."

"Not our doc," came a voice from the open door. "He'd never harm an animal."

Both Dixie and Michael looked up. A woman with thick blond hair braided over her shoulder smiled. Her eyes flashed as Michael swooped forward to pick her up in his arms. He spun her around as she laughed. Once her feet hit the ground, she let her arms drop from his neck, giving his cheek a kiss.

"You're back," he said, still grinning at her.

"My last final is done," she said, nodding. "One more semester and I graduate."

He turned to Dixie. "This is Sage McCloud, Meadow's daughter. She's home for Christmas."

"So I see," mumbled Dixie. *Now isn't this the chummy reunion. I don't care if she's beautiful and Meadow's offspring. She was too quick to defend the doc. If there's such a thing as a Young Rocker, she'd be one.* Dixie looked her up and down, as if she were a suspect.

When Meadow mentioned a daughter, I thought she'd be

early twenties. But now I see that she's older than I thought. Closer to my age. Doesn't look much like her mother. Smaller and more compact. Blue eyes. Dixie sighed. *Speaking of which, I wouldn't object if he wanted to swing me in the air like that.*

Michael continued. "Sage, this is Dixie Jones. Meadow probably already told you Dixie's been staying with her while she's visiting Lily Rock."

Sage nodded a greeting to Dixie. "Yes, she told me. Nice to meet you." Hands on hips, Sage looked over the storage shed. "Mom said I'd find you here when I called her while I was driving back from college. I thought I'd stop here first since it's on the way home. Looking for the baby Jesus?" The corner of her mouth twitched.

"By some miracle he didn't get burned in the fire," Michael explained.

Sage's smile disappeared. "I heard about Lola's and old man Maguire. Gosh, I'll miss him and that place. The doc took me there for my first beer when I turned twenty-one."

"How old are you?" Dixie asked.

"I'm thirty-four. I know what you're thinking, that I'm too old to be in college. I went back late to finish a degree I started over a decade ago. There was some talk in town that I could get a job at the music academy, so I decided to finish the rest of my education. I'd love that job."

Dixie smiled. *I'm just a few years older, but we have more in common than I thought. Two women going back to school to make a change in their lives.*

Sage pointed to the open box. "So what did you find in there?"

"Enough drugs to put the entire town of Lily Rock to sleep," muttered Dixie.

"Have you noticed," Michael began, "that it's gotten really

quiet at Paws and Pines? There used to be dogs barking day and night."

"A couple of them finally yipped at the motorcycle gang," Dixie admitted. "But that's all I've heard and we've been here for nearly two hours."

Dixie raised her finger in the air to call for quiet and listen.

After a pause, Sage shrugged. "I mostly come up here to exercise the horses for Doc. It's been a while since I was last home. But now that you mention it, I don't remember hearing the dogs last time or the time before that."

"Do you think you could get us access to the kennels? It's possible that most of the animals got adopted, you know, for Christmas."

"That would account for less barking," Michael admitted.

Sage reached for her phone. "I can ask Brad if we can visit the dogs and cats. Give me a minute." She texted and hit Send. A ping came right back. Sage read from her screen. "I guess they've locked up for the night, earlier than usual because it's Christmas Eve." Sage frowned.

Dixie kept staring at Sage. *I think I like this woman. She took charge and made that phone call. She's not making excuses for Lily Rock.*

"So let's get going." Dixie pulled her crutches close to her body. "I've got another idea."

Sage stood by the door, waiting for her to pass. "For someone who's just visiting, I'm surprised you're taking such an interest in the animal shelter."

Dixie lifted her crutches, swinging her body out of the doorway. "I led your mother to believe that I'm a tourist looking for a Christmas getaway."

"But you're not..." Sage's voice trailed off.

When they all stood outside the shed, Sage asked, "So you're not a visitor?"

Michael smirked.

Dixie blurted out, "I am a cop and I can't say much more. A need-to-know kind of thing. But I will tell you that my name isn't Dixie Jones."

Michael spoke up. "So what is your real name? I may want to send you a gift card for the holidays." His eyebrow lifted.

Both Michael and Sage stared at her, waiting to hear what she had to say. *I like these two and I have to say it surprises me.*

She cleared her throat. "My captain will kill me, but I'm going to tell you anyway. My name is Janis Jets. I'm the cop sent to find out who's been sending anonymous emails and what's up with Lily Rock." When Michael smiled and Sage nodded, she grinned back.

Now they know and no one's overly upset. It's like they expected me, like they knew I'd be coming. Maybe not me personally, but somebody like me. She looked them over more closely for telltale signs of discomfort. Michael shifted his gaze to look at the ceiling. Sage's lips drew a straight line as her eyes darted here and there. *Yep, they suspected.*

Janis hoisted the crutches under her arms. "Time to get going. We have to report back to Meadow before the tree lighting ceremony." She shoved her crutches ahead of her, swinging her legs forward.

Ouch.

Who knew sore armpits could be so debilitating.

17

MEADOW DOES THE DISHES

Sage beat them back to Meadow's, the first one to open her front door, rolling her suitcase next to her. Michael came next, with Janis Jets struggling with her crutches, dragging her booted leg alongside her. Meadow greeted Sage with a warm hug. "How were your finals, dear?" She stepped back to inspect her daughter's face.

"Finals were fine. I'm so happy to be home." Sage rolled in a suitcase and made her way down the hall. She called back over her shoulder, "I'll dump this stuff and see you in a minute."

Janis Jets cleared her throat. "I want to get this off my chest right away. So Meadow, you may want to kick me out of your spare room when you hear this..."

Meadow's eyes twinkled. "I'm so happy you've decided to come clean. You were too curious to be an insurance adjuster."

Janis shot her an admiring glance. *She's no dummy.*

"So are you a barista or a dog walker or a professor?" Meadow asked.

Jets shook her head. "That's a variety of things I'd never be. In fact, I'm a cop. I'm training at the police academy, but I came with years of small-town experience in another state. So they asked me to show up undercover in Lily Rock. There were anonymous emails and the request for police presence."

Meadow's face froze. Jets immediately stopped explaining. *So she doesn't want police presence in Lily Rock and my true identity makes her react like this. I don't think she knew anything about the emails. Just look at her face.*

Michael cleared his throat. "Maybe we can talk about all of that later." His eyes darted to Janis.

He noticed Meadow's reaction too... Janis looked around the living room. She shifted on her crutches, feeling a throb moving its way up her leg. "Maybe I'd better sit down for a bit..."

"Let's elevate that foot," Meadow agreed. Michael took her by the elbow, ushering her to the sofa. Before she could sit down, Sage returned to the living room and pulled a chair closer to the sofa. Janis lost her balance, plopping down on the sofa, her crutches snatched out of the air by Michael's capable hands. She turned her body around, stretching her booted leg in front of her. "Not very graceful," she admitted with a shrug.

Meadow slipped a pillow onto the chair. "There you go," she said, helping Janis rest her ankle on top. She felt an immediate release of tension as she fell back into the sofa cushions.

"Much better," she mumbled. Meadow turned away.

Michael bent over to whisper in her ear. "We can talk about the emails later, when Meadow isn't around." Then he walked across the room to sit next to Sage on the loveseat.

Does he know more about this than I thought...

"I'm fixing a light supper for us, so I'll leave you to it," Meadow announced. When she turned to walk into the kitchen, Janis took the moment to consider her options. She eyed Michael and Sage. He set his face in a bemused expression, while Sage looked at her fingernails. *They both look guilty. The secret is in their court now.*

Jets cleared her throat. She heard preparations being made from the kitchen. Convinced Meadow couldn't hear, she glared at Michael and Sage from across the room. Plus she had a hunch. It wasn't just those two but someone else, a third party, who'd gotten involved.

Sage looked up with wide eyes. Michael stared at his knees.

"I want to talk to you two and Marla Osbourne as well. A nice little chat. Face to face so that we can get all chummy." They both squirmed. *Bingo. Gotcha.* She smiled, feeling the situation was now in hand.

First she looked at Michael. "Do you think Marla would come over on short notice?"

"Maybe," he said, "but what do you want to talk to her about?"

She hesitated, mostly to watch him squirm. Then she cleared her throat again. "I want to discuss those emails, and I don't care if Meadow knows."

The academy insisted that speaking the truth firmly, without flinching, sped up the confessions. Michael's eyes darted at her again. Sage made herself small, leaning back into the cushions. Now she was the one staring at her knees.

Janis shrugged. *Okay, so let's try another approach.* She altered her tone to sound more encouraging. "Let's just say I'd like to have you and Sage, along with Marla, help me brainstorm."

"Did someone commit a crime?" Sage asked.

"We have a dead body," Jets reminded her.

"You don't think someone killed old man Maguire, do you?" asked Michael.

Look at them deflecting. "I would like the assurance that the old guy died accidentally of smoke inhalation and that the fire was not arson. When I file my report, I'll recommend that the arson squad have a look and that an autopsy be done on the body."

"Will you be the person to do the investigating?" Sage asked.

"I don't know," she admitted. *But there's another problem here, something I realized just today.* "Paws and Pines Animal Shelter stores boxes of medications in their back shed. Put that together with how quiet the shelter is, I think the captain would agree to a further investigation. Of course we'd need a warrant to get into the kennel. Searching for the baby Jesus isn't enough to get a warrant on its own."

"Just so you know, Marla already tried to report the shelter to the Riverside police months ago."

Jets's stomach twisted. *I could extend my stay in Lily Rock. Settle this case. Let my ankle heal.* She looked at Michael. He looked back. She hesitated. This time she didn't feel the quiver of attraction in her stomach. His eyes didn't make her wonder about kissing him. Instead she felt a friendliness, but nothing more. A different reaction, not unpleasant but definitely not as heated.

"Call Marla," she snapped at Michael. "She can try to report the shelter again. Enough chitchat." She grimaced. Her ankle throbbed.

"Another pain pill, dear?" Meadow stood in the kitchen doorway.

Jets sighed. "Sorry, I'm feeling a bit cranky. No more pills. I have to be able to think clearly."

Next thing you know I'll be living in Lily Rock, opening a constabulary on Main Street. Then after I'm done with parking tickets and giving warrants to tourists for not picking up the dog poop, I'll be having this crew over for coffee. What's happened to me? It must be the pain meds.

* * *

After some soft talk and encouragement over the phone, Michael managed to persuade Marla Osbourne to join them for dinner.

"Come on, Marla. We can talk to Dixie, I mean Janis. And then we'll eat with our friends and then go to the tree lighting. It will be fun. Give you a chance to get out of that trailer and mingle. You know that would make you feel better."

Once he clicked off the phone, he told Janis and Sage, "She's coming over right now. Unfortunately she's been kind of reclusive lately. Not feeling well. Her allergies are kicking up."

"I have a special tea for that," Meadow said before disappearing back into the kitchen.

Jets closed her eyes to rest as Michael and Sage whispered together on the love seat. Her eyes flew open when Meadow announced, "Soup's on," from the doorway.

With Michael's help she raised from the sofa. He offered his arm. "I'll help you to the kitchen." She nodded, disregarding the crutches nearby.

In the kitchen Meadow scooped soup into bowls. The sight of fresh-baked bread and slices of fruit at each setting made Janis's stomach growl. With help from Michael, she sat down, her leg extended under the table. A knock came from the front door. Michael excused himself, saying, "I'll get it," and disappeared into the living room.

Janis heard voices. Then Michael and Marla stood in the doorway. He stepped closer to pull out her chair, and as Marla sat down, he sat next to her. Michael leaned over the table to ladle soup into her bowl at the same time as Sage shoved the bread basket toward them.

Jets observed Marla and Michael. She felt a tingle in her gut. *There's something out of kilter with those two. She keeps looking at him as if she needs reassurance.*

"One more thing," Meadow announced. She stood up and took something from the counter. A tall chocolate cake smothered in thick chocolate buttercream frosting was set at the center of the table. Meadow passed around plates and forks.

* * *

"That was delicious," Marla said. "Thanks for inviting me. I've been a bit reclusive lately." Her voice quivered slightly.

"We understand, dear." Meadow stood up. "I have some dishes to do. Why don't the rest of you chat while I tidy up." She walked away from the table toward the far end of the kitchen.

As soon as the water rushed into the sink, Janis spoke. "So which one of you sent those emails to the Riverside Precinct about the need for police presence in Lily Rock?" She made a point of pausing to look at each face carefully, expecting tell-tale signs.

Michael stared straight ahead. Sage's eyes grew wide. She pointed to Meadow's back and then put her finger over her lips.

Marla frowned and whispered, "It was my idea. There's something not right here. I sent the first email to the Riverside police after I talked to Sage and Michael. When I got an automatic response, I sent two more. Finally someone replied and said they'd look into it."

Sage looked nervously toward her mother's back. When

Meadow didn't turn around she held her finger over her lips again. "Keep explaining, just keep it quiet."

Marla continued, "I've been doing some ancestry research on the library computer. I found I have roots in Lily Rock, so I started asking around. People were uncomfortable, especially Doc May. Then I got a creepy feeling like people were watching me."

Michael held up his hand. "So she asked me to be her bodyguard, only pretend we were a couple."

That explains it. They're not really together. "Besides a creepy feeling, did anything actually happen to you?" Janis asked.

"Probably allergies," Marla said. Then her jaw tightened. "But the town is off. What with the bikers and the bad tourist reviews on social media. I mentioned that in one of my emails. I'm kind of psychic and I get feelings about this kind of thing."

The flow of water stopped. Meadow returned, wrinkles appearing on her forehead. "Oh, I forgot to pick up the bread plates." She gathered them, returning to the sink.

When the water started running again, Jets nodded to Sage. "What was your role in all of this?"

"I helped Marla write the emails, but I don't want the Old Rockers to know, especially my mom. They think they've got everything under control."

"The town is changing," muttered Marla. "Even I can see that."

Meadow turned off the water again. She hurried across the room to ask, "Does anyone want tea with their cake?"

"I'll take whatever you've got," Janis said, hoping Meadow would get busy again and leave her to ask more questions of the other three.

"I have the perfect blend to help you relax and heal." Meadow nodded.

Janis took inventory of her suspects and their reactions. They looked more at ease. Less tense. Each one gave her direct eye contact. Michael even smiled.

With the three of them having admitted to the emails and to keeping them a secret from Meadow, the captain could not complain now. He'd assigned her the task of getting to the bottom of the emails. She'd deliver, with three confessions. A sigh of relief escaped her lips.

Janis had to admit, *If Michael knew about the request for police presence and the emails, maybe he figured out right away that I might be undercover.*

Years later, when Janis would recollect how they first met, she'd remember this very conversation. How they ate soup and hid the truth from Meadow. How they all became friends, even Marla. And especially the first taste of that chocolate cake.

Janis's eyes closed as she savored the last lick of chocolate on her lip.

"I have to leave you for a few more minutes," Meadow announced. "While you were at the shelter I made up a basket for the baby Jesus. I'll fill it with straw to look more authentic."

"Jesus was born in a desert in the summer equinox," Sage said dryly.

"Oh I know, dear. But that doesn't mean we can't celebrate in the winter, now does it? It's all a metaphor anyway. The sign of something new coming in the least expected way."

"We could use something new here in Lily Rock," Sage agreed, looking directly at Janis.

18

MAGUIRE

It was nine o'clock by the time they stood in the center of town. Michael held Marla's arm. Sage, hands shoved in the pockets of her puffy coat, looked into the woods where Lola's used to be. Janis Jets leaned against both crutches.

She felt a bite of cold on her nose. Looking up, flakes of snow drifted in the sky, some floating to the ground. Over the pine trees and the sequoias, the moon rose, the air feeling still and otherworldly. Janis shivered, sticking out her tongue.

"Nothing like the first snow," Michael said with a smile.

"Perfect timing," Marla agreed. Then she pointed. "Is that the tree for the lighting celebration?"

A three-foot straggly pine sat leaning slightly to the left. An extension cord trailed across the street. Meadow held the plug in her hand.

"Mom told me they would use the electrical from the library," Sage commented.

"Probably another fire hazard," mumbled Jets. She looked at the four connected extension cords and shook her head.

People gathered near the tree. Others walked down the

middle of Main Street dressed in jackets, mittens, and every style of hat. Boots trudged against the boardwalk. Footprints in the street marked where the snow had begun to accumulate.

Janis turned to Michael. "Quiet has its own sound," she said. "Maybe the only time I feel remotely relaxed."

Michael looked down at her. "Look at you going all deep. Next thing you know, you'll be singing 'Silent Night' and acting happy."

"Never gonna happen," she muttered.

Voices grew louder from the crowd huddling together near the small tree. Gentle laughter and a child pointing to the basket next to the tree caught Janis's attention. The mother leaned over to whisper in her ear.

"Mom was right. The kids care about Jesus in the manger."

An oversized wicker basket filled with straw stood near the tree. A big red and green bow tied on the handle made it look festive. Janis nodded. "She's good with ribbon."

"I'll tell her you said so," Sage giggled. "Just wait until Labor Day. You'll get the full effect of Meadow's ribbon expertise. She has this hat..."

A low rumble coming from the distance interrupted her explanation. Janis, remembering the sound from the day before, knew the source. Motorcycles rolled past, two abreast, underneath the *Welcome to Lily Rock* sign.

They kept a slow and steady pace to give pedestrians the opportunity to cross the street on their way to the tree lighting ceremony. The lead motorcycle stopped and held up his hand. The rest of the bikes stayed behind him. His engine revved, an encouragement for the people to hurry. A few stragglers scampered past, heading toward the rest of the crowd.

Janis watched the bikers carefully. Her eyes were drawn to a woman who sat behind the lead rider on his bike. She wore a leather jacket and tight-fitting jeans, plus boots to her knees. Her helmet covered her face, her hair streaming down her back. Shoved between her and the man was a blanket bundle. Her arms were extended around the blanket to clasp her hands at the man's waist.

Once everyone had crossed, he lowered his hand and then revved his engine again. The other motorcycles followed from behind, rolling toward the tree. Gathering in a semicircle, they spaced themselves apart. From Janis's point of view, the motorcycle riders encompassed the rest of the onlookers. She might have felt uncomfortable but the situation did not set off any alarms.

Jets leaned toward Michael. "Do they always show up for the tree lighting?"

"Actually they do. But I think this time it's about showing their respect for old man Maguire."

Janis shivered. "Are they gonna start singing and holding hands?"

Sage laughed. "You got that right. This is Lily Rock's answer to *The Grinch Who Stole Christmas*. Remember? All the Who down in Whoville stood in a circle and sang..."

"Lily Rock isn't a child's picture book. There are real problems here," Janis said quietly. No one bothered to disagree. Despite her initial lack of alarm, she still bristled at their lack of worldly concern. She felt defiance sweep over her.

I feel responsible for this town. I feel edgy and angry for them. They take unnecessary risks and refuse to see potential danger that could be avoided, if they only woke up.

Surprised at her own feelings, she shrugged. Before she could consider her thoughts further a hush came over the crowd. One of the bikers, helmet left on his seat, walked forward. He wore thick leathers and scuffed boots. He held something in his arms, wrapped in a blanket.

Walking closer to the wicker basket, he bent over to place the bundle inside. His big hand reached underneath to pull straw from the bottom of the basket. He spread it over the top of the bundle, then stood up. Bowing his head for a moment, he turned and walked back to his motorcycle, as the rest of the gang and the crowd watched in silence.

At that moment from across the street, Meadow plugged in the extension cord. The small tree lit up. There was no gasp from the crowd because the small tree didn't evoke such a response. It looked pathetic and alone. The crowd stayed quiet, and disappointment hung in the air.

The only decoration on the tree was a sprinkling of snow across the spindly branches. Jets pulled on Michael's arm. "This isn't the usual reaction, right?"

"No, it isn't. Meadow must be disappointed."

"But what about the biker guy? Did he bring the missing baby Jesus? That should cheer people up. Looks like he had the statue all along."

Michael nodded, his eyes still on the tree and the basket.

Janis felt a stirring in the crowd. "Is that it? The tree lighting ceremony is over?"

"It's about done," Sage mumbled.

"Hey, wait a minute." Marla frowned. "Take a look at baby Jesus. That bundle. It's moving!" Her voice carried in the cold night, as other heads looked to where she pointed.

Soon the entire crowd stared at the basket. "Is it baby Jesus, Mom?" came a small child's voice. The bundle began to wobble side to side, nearing tipping over.

"Did those guys bring us a real baby?" Jets exclaimed. She hitched her crutches toward her body.

Michael held up his hand. "You stay there. Sage and I will get closer to figure things out."

"You people are nuts," Jets added, feeling alarm in her gut. "That could be a stolen baby. Who knows what that gang would do to make a point. Maybe they've gone and found a real baby when you couldn't come up with the plastic one."

Michael along with Sage walked toward the tree as the rest of the crowd watched. They approached the basket. By now it had tipped on its side, straw falling into the dirt. The blanket moved, making Jets squeamish. *Maybe a raccoon... Please just not a human child.* Jets watched carefully as Sage leaned over to look inside.

The crowd took in a collective breath, waiting for her assessment.

Sage bent her knees to get closer to the bundle. She used both hands to scoop it up, turning to face Michael. He pulled away the cover to peer inside. Then he looked away before facing the crowd.

Even from a distance Jets could see his eyes glisten with tears.

Sage tucked the blanket around the bundle, wrapping in the corners. Michael walked beside her as they came closer to Jets. "Guess what?" he said, a huge smile on his face. "The baby Jesus showed up after all."

Fearing the worst, Jets shook her head. People crowded around as the bundle wriggled in Sage's arms. Michael tugged gently at the corner of the blanket with his fingers, releasing it from Sage's grip.

"Look what we have here," he said. Lifting the bundle in his arms, the blanket fell away, revealing a squirming mass of curly brown fur, four paws, and a black button nose. A tail wagged as it yipped hello.

"A dog!" Janis Jets said aloud. "It's a puppy, not a person. Oh thank you, divine matrix of being."

"What?" Sage looked quizzical.

"Your old man God in the sky by another name," she commented dryly and then added, "Hand over the pup. I am so relieved."

The crowd drew closer. The puppy's cold nose rubbed against the inside of Janis's elbow as his tail wagged with happiness.

"What do you think? Around ten weeks old?" Janis scratched behind his ears.

Meadow glanced at the bundle and then called out to the crowd. "We've been given a new puppy. What will we name him?"

People looked from one to the other as everyone considered Meadow's question. A few suggestions were shouted aloud, and then the right one made everyone nod.

"Okay then," Meadow said. She reached for the puppy. "I'll take him home and get a tag made right away." She lowered her nose to rub his. Then she looked out at the crowd. "Does everyone think that's the name?"

All heads nodded in agreement.

Meadow raised her arms, holding the puppy in the air. His furry legs dangled, his tail quivering. His tongue slipped from the side of his mouth. "Here he is, our Lily Rock dog. We will name him Maguire."

Cheers went up from the bikers as everyone else joined in. Meadow lowered the squirming dog from the air, holding him closer to her body. Sage stepped up to wrap Maguire in the soft blanket. "I'll take him home for now," Meadow said. "But we can share him. One home to another until he's old enough to pick his family."

Jets laughed.

"What's so funny?" Michael turned to her.

"You people are crazy. Nobody does that with a dog. Maguire can't pick his own family."

"We'll see about that." Meadow leaned over to plant a kiss on Maguire's furry head.

19

CHRISTMAS BUNS

On Christmas morning, dressed and packed, Janis Jets stood in the bedroom looking around. She shivered. Stepping closer to the window, she pulled aside the curtain.

Snow covered the ground. Bright soft snow, the kind in children's books. She sighed. Bumping her suitcase on the floor with her crutch, she rolled it closer to the door. With one hand she shoved the suitcase into the hallway. Soft music played in the living room.

Janis stood next to her bag and sniffed. *Come on. Cinnamon rolls on Christmas morning? Meadow is too much.* Putting a bit of weight on her boot, she winced. She rested a hand along the wall for balance, leaving her bag by the open door to the guest room.

"Merry Christmas, dear," came Meadow's voice from the living room. Janis took the few steps from the hallway to the living room where she found Meadow wearing a faded pair of denim jeans with a bright red tunic that came to her knees. Red earrings made to look like a wrapped package hung from both ears. A red and green plaid apron was tied around her neck and waist. Meadow looked like an overgrown elf.

"Good morning. Merry Christmas," Janis mumbled, but just to be polite.

Sage stuck her head into the living room from the kitchen doorway. "We've got juice and fresh buns from the oven." She smirked as Janis rolled her eyes. "Come sit yourself down. So much to talk about."

A sharp yip came from the kitchen.

"The dog," Janis said. "I completely forgot about Maguire."

"He's eating his breakfast," Meadow said, taking her by the arm. "Come see."

They followed the sound of puppy yipping. Stepping into the kitchen, Janis noticed the newspaper that covered the floor. A wire corral circled around one side of the kitchen, the dog inside next to an enormous metal food bowl. He wagged his tail, poking his paw at the bowl.

Even more newspapers had been strewn over the floor inside the makeshift enclosure. One showed a wet spot. "Potty training," Janis mumbled. "I want to pet him, but I can't bend over without falling." She stared at her injured ankle.

"So sit here." Meadow pulled out a chair. "Sage will bring him to you. It will give me a chance to freshen up the newspaper."

Once seated, Janis waited. Sage bent over to grab the puppy, holding him close to her body. She smiled and tickled him behind his ears. "There you go, Maguire. Remember Dixie Jones from last night?" Sage looked at her and then corrected herself. "I mean Janis Jets. You remember her from last night."

Sage came closer. Holding out the puppy, she placed him on Janis's lap. He tottered over her knees, his front paws reaching for the floor. Janis wrapped her arms around the furry bundle to keep him from falling.

He spun in her lap and put his paws on Janis's chest and licked her mouth.

"Hey, stop that," Jets growled. She wouldn't admit it to anyone, but she actually liked being licked.

As Meadow and Sage bustled around the enclosure, Janis held the puppy. He'd turned to face the room, his body leaning into her chest, his head cocked to the side. "Do you think he wants to go outside?" Janis asked.

When no one answered, she said louder, "Do you think Maguire wants to go outside?" She used his name; he looked back at her.

"Maguire already knows his name," came a voice from the doorway. Michael Bellemare stood, tall and handsome, smiling at Janis. "Merry Christmas," he said brightly, reaching for the puppy. "I'll take him outside."

As soon as Maguire was taken from her, Janis's lap felt empty. She wanted to take him out herself, but her ankle prevented her from making an honest effort. She felt a tingle of sadness but was then interrupted by Meadow's bright voice. "Here you go." She left a large glass of orange juice in front of her.

Janis drank gratefully as Meadow watched. "I have coffee if you're ready."

"Oh, I'd like that." The sadness instantly evaporated.

Within minutes Michael came through the back door, holding Maguire in his arms, a leash dangling from the puppy's collar. "He pooped!"

Sage and Meadow applauded.

"Give me a break," groaned Janis.

Michael put the puppy back in the enclosure. He pulled a cookie shaped like a dog bone from his pocket, which Maguire snatched out of his hand. "He takes treats. That's a good sign,"

Michael said. He walked across the room toward the table, pulling out the chair next to Janis.

"So how's the ankle this morning?"

She looked him over carefully before speaking. He'd gone outside without his jacket. A sprinkle of snow lay on his shoulders, lightly dusting the front of his flannel shirt. He ran his hand through his hair self-consciously, as if he knew she was checking him out. "My hair okay?" he asked.

Janis waited for the rise of heat she'd come to expect when in his presence. When it didn't come, her eyes narrowed. "You're fine," she told him. Her heart did not flutter, nor did she feel close to blushing. *Is the magic gone?*

He openly stared at her, as if he'd sensed something different between them. He cleared his throat. Right then Meadow shoved a basket with a stack of gigantic cinnamon rolls between them. She waved it under his nose.

"Christmas buns," she announced. "Have as many as you want. I only bake them once a year."

Jets and Michael both reached for buns from the basket. Covered in gooey frosting, she held it to her nose and then sank her teeth into the warm goodness. She took her time enjoying it before she swallowed. "So where's Marla? I thought Christmas morning would be spent with you doing some early morning bodyguarding."

"I'm off duty." He licked his fingers and then took another bite. "Plus Marla and I are pretty sick of each other, living in such close proximity."

She expected to be more excited by this revelation, but she wasn't. She took another bite of warm cinnamon roll. *How come this doughy goodness attracts me more than hunky Bellemare?*

By the time Sage and Meadow joined them, Janis had finished her roll and reached for another. The happy chatter back and forth over the table made her feel comfortable. She didn't interrupt their easy kidding, feeling relaxed, a feeling she'd come to recognize since her stay in Lily Rock. *I like these people. They feel good to me. Like I've landed in a family or something. But I know I can't be a good cop for Lily Rock; I've gotten too close.*

After she finished her second bun, Janis rubbed her sticky fingers on the napkin and spoke. "I'm well enough to drive down the hill today with my good foot. Traffic should be light since it's a holiday. Just want to tell all of you it's been a real experience here in Lily Rock. I'll let you know when I file my report." Shocked faces made her gut clench. *Too much cinnamon roll*, she told herself.

She scooted her chair backward. Putting her weight on her good leg, she lifted herself out of the chair. Walking slowly through the doorway into the living room, she did not turn back. She didn't want to see their faces again.

Janis dragged and scooted down the hallway to grab her suitcase. She rolled it to the front door. When no one came to say goodbye she mumbled under her breath, "Merry Christmas, you crazy Lily Rock people. It's been nice knowing you." The door closed softly behind her.

20

WELCOME TO LILY ROCK

Sitting behind the wheel, she executed a couple of quick leg lifts. *Not too painful. I'll be able to use my good foot to brake and accelerate.* She pulled her car away from the house and made her way to the main road. Driving slowly, she inhaled the crisp air from her open window, smelling the pine and a waft of burning wood. She didn't feel alarmed, associating the smell with Christmas logs in fireplaces.

A glance in the rearview mirror revealed no other vehicles. She sighed. *And here I thought they might come after me. Oh well. They know this was a job and that I'd have to go sometime.*

Once in town she pulled to the side of the road, right under the *Welcome to Lily Rock* sign. Phone in hand, she placed a call. The captain barked into her ear. "I have a day off. Unless you're on fire, call me tomorrow!"

"Wait a minute," she told him before he could hang up. "I'm driving home. As soon as I get in the door I'll send a report." She thought of her cold apartment where she'd be alone with her thoughts. No one to share the day with, not even a soft warm puppy to cuddle.

"Okay then, fill me in quick. Tell me what you found out." His voice sounded slightly less barbed.

"Three Lily Rock residents were responsible for those emails. They were in cahoots." She didn't bother to name the culprits. "They had their reasons for making it anonymous. This is a small town, and there's a group called the Old Rockers who might have taken offense."

"Stop it!" he yelled. "None of that we're-only-a-small-town nonsense. Just the facts."

"I think a coroner's report about the dead body might be in order. But it looks and feels like an accident. So does the fire. Probably someone's motorcycle sparked and lit up the weeds nearby. It's dry up here until the first snow. Quite a blaze. You might be able to get someone for unintentional arson due to negligence, but you'd have trouble finding out which bike it was."

When the captain didn't say anything, Jets kept talking. "For the record, they found out I'm a cop."

"Did they now?" He sounded as if he'd already suspected. "Did you tell them?"

She wanted to deny that she'd given up her undercover identity. *So unprofessional.* But she didn't want to make up a lie either. So she affirmed his suspicions. "I told them. Had to—they'd figured it out already."

"And you got too close to the very people you were sent to observe. Rookie mistake." He didn't hold back the sound of condemnation in his voice.

Jets sighed. "Yes, sir." *Even I can't argue with that.*

His gruff voice broke the silence. "Are we done yet? I have a turkey to baste and another call coming through. Isn't it supposed to be a sacred holiday?"

"Are you religious, sir?" she asked.

"I believe in the religion of love, Jets. Plus I'm hanging up now. Goodbye."

She tossed her cell on the passenger seat and adjusted her knee with both hands. Once comfortable she glanced into the rearview mirror. To her surprise, Michael Bellemare's truck had pulled up behind her. He was talking into his cell. He grinned and waved. She dipped her head, hiding a smirk.

In a minute her passenger-side door opened. He leaned in and grabbed her cell off the seat. Then he sat down, slamming the door and handing the phone back to her.

"Who were you talking to on your cell?" Suspicion came with Janis's question.

He hid a grin. "The LA police force must work twenty-four seven. I was speaking to the captain. Your captain, in fact."

"So you're best friends now?"

"He's kind of a tough guy," Michael answered.

She poked his arm. "And how would you know that?"

"Oh, I called him a day ago and we chatted a long time. I wanted to ask if you were who I thought you were—you know, a cop."

"Did he tell you I am still at the academy and this assignment was his big idea?"

"Not at first, but eventually I wore him down."

Caps never said he outed me before I outed myself. I'm gonna have a word with him tomorrow. Looks like the rookie mistake is on him.

Michael turned his body to face her. If it had been earlier, she'd have expected him to move closer and finally deliver that long-awaited kiss. When nothing happened, her inner voice took over. *Come on, Janis. You know he's hot.*

She waited but still no zing. She felt a certain warmth and okay, a great fondness for Michael, but nothing more. Whatever she'd felt earlier was gone. When Michael didn't make a move, she broke the silence.

"So I gotta go. Heading back down the hill."

He chuckled. "Well that's the thing. You see, I know something that your captain may not have told you. He decided on the phone just now."

Hair rose on her neck. "I doubt that."

"Let's just say, it's Christmas and I want to save you a trip." He scratched behind his ear. "Plus you have a broken ankle. I think it's a bit unsafe to be driving just yet."

"What are you talking about?"

"So I swore to your captain that I wouldn't tell you first. But my fingers were crossed." He held them in the air as if to prove his point. "Congratulations, you're being assigned to Lily Rock permanently. Your captain is going to personally oversee your last semester at the academy so that you can get to work with a field training officer for the next few months. He calls it a hybrid training, like student teaching. Then you move to Lily Rock. Our first official police presence.

"The Old Rockers will agree tomorrow," Michael kept talking. "Meadow is already on board. They will talk to Arlo and Cay out of courtesy, but they won't object.

"Once I show the Old Rockers my plan to refurbish an old rental next to the library for a new constabulary, I know they'll be all for it. And then we'll be ready to move you in. It will be basic at first. But after a while we'll build a state-of-the-art facility with glass doors and surveillance. Cells with programmable keypads. The works."

"What are you talking about?" Janis shook her head.

He stared at her. "You want this. You know you do."

Her jaw clenched. *I don't like it when people tell me what I do and don't want. Kind of...* But before she could object, she had to admit he was right.

The minute I ran into that burning building all my doubts about being a small-town cop were gone. When I got here I thought I'd made a mistake and that small towns would be a waste of time. Until I rushed into that building...

She looked over at Michael. *It was never about my feelings toward Lily Rock. It was about their feelings for me. They picked me almost from the moment I walked into the library and Meadow offered me a place to stay.*

She reached over, patting his cheek as if he were a schoolboy needing a compliment. "Okay then. I guess it's all settled. I'm moving to Lily Rock."

He looked a bit surprised. "I thought it would take more persuasion."

She grinned. "But just so you know, the two of us?" She pointed to him and then to herself. "We're not a thing. We might have been at one time."

"You mean that you no longer find me attractive?" His eyes grew wide with playful dismay. He looked more amused than upset. Then he shrugged. "I know what you mean. It's like we're meant to be close, but just friends." A faraway look came over his eyes, his face filled with longing.

But that look isn't for me.

"But I do feel like I've always known you," she told him. "And here I thought you were a one-night stand, but it looks like there's more to it than that." She patted his shoulder. "All of this kind of reminds me of that old movie with Humphrey Bogart."

His eyes lit up. "With Claude Rains! *Casablanca* is one of my top ten films. I'm Bogart, of course."

"Just remember I'm the cop." Her chin jutted out.

He glanced out the windshield. Her eyes followed his gaze. Snow had accumulated on the hood of her truck, flakes still drifting from above. When he turned to face her, his eyes were warm. "Let's just say what we've got here—"

"Is the beginning of a beautiful friendship," she finished his sentence.

Their eyes met. Both nodded in agreement.

"Okay then, since there's no hurry, let's turn around and go back to Meadow's. I'm having another cinnamon roll for lunch. I'm also going to pet Maguire. What are you gonna do?"

"Follow you and do the same. Once the snow melts we'll find you a place. And by the way." He pointed to the sign overhead. "Welcome to Lily Rock."

Prologue

Overheard in Lily Rock

"I love the town of Lily Rock. Their lies are so authentic."

Fog rolled over the mountain road. Despite the poor visibility, the woman drove as if her life depended upon it.

A sharp curve to the right—her squealing tires issued a warning.

Tentatively removing one hand from the steering wheel, she kept her eyes on the road, her fingers reaching down for her windshield wipers. *Swish.* The blade on the glass moved to the left, then the right. Her gaze remained fixed on the road in front of her. Reaching over the steering wheel, she swiped with her hand at the thick condensation blocking her view from inside the car.

Veering into the next curve, she felt her stomach lurch. Brakes squealed again as the car catapulted into an unexpected second hairpin turn. Her head lolled to the right. As she came out of the curve, she pushed the button on the foggy driver's side door and rolled down the window, revealing clouds of fog.

Another vehicle rumbled behind her car, close to her bumper.

"I guess somebody's in a big hurry," she snapped to the empty car.

The window slid shut as she looked out of the front windshield to the right, then the left. No turnout lane yet. Tightness stiffened her neck as her hands began to shake on the wheel. *Stop tailgating me. Please.*

She felt the tires slip on the road, the car floating for a moment. As she slammed on the brakes, her body heaved against the seat belt, her neck and head rocking forward then back. Her stomach came up to her throat.

As her car skidded toward the cliff, she only had one thought:

I finally know how I will die.

End of Sample
**To continue reading Getway Death, pick up a
copy at your favorite retailer.**

GET A FREE SHORT STORY

Join my VIP newsletter to get the latest news of Lily Rock along with contests, discounts, events, and giveaways! I'll also send you *Meadow's Hat*, a short story set before book one :).

Sign up on bonniehardywrites.com/newsletter

ACKNOWLEDGMENTS

Holiday stories have filled an important part of my life for as long as I can remember. Louisa May Alcott's *Little Women* begins with Jo's comment, "Christmas won't be Christmas without any presents."

Yet Christmas comes to the March sisters right on time, despite their limited circumstances.

That's the piece I hope to capture in my first holiday novella. The sense of celebration and hope in the midst of the challenge of everyday events.

After writing five *Lily Rock Mysteries* I developed a curiosity about my characters' backstories. Once the stories were written in the first novella, I knew I had to write more prequels. You can expect the next holiday book to be available by the fall of 2023, when Janis Jets and Michael Bellemare, Meadow and Sage, and the rest of the town get together again.

So here is the first in a series of holiday books about the beloved town of Lily Rock.

Again I'd like to thank my team of helpers, who assist me in creating the best book possible for my readers. Christie Stratos at Proof Positive for her expert editing. Dane and his crew at Ebook Launch who bring to life my characters and settings with their imaginative flair for drawing and art. And finally thanks to Kate Tilton who manages all the details of independent publishing and who has just the right suggestion ready for me, at exactly the right time.

Of course my small dynamic family, Bill and Emily,

deserve all of my thanks. They stand by me as I write, edit, and write again. And they never bat an eye when I talk about the fictional family in Lily Rock, as if they were part of the family.

And I'd like to thank you dear readers, for your questions and engagement with the books. The imagination is a powerful place to share our greatest love and concerns. I'm grateful that we can do this together.

Happy Holidays!
Bonnie

ABOUT THE AUTHOR

My name is Bonnie Hardy and I write the kind of books I like to read.

I love a good cozy mystery. From the cover art to the first page, I can barely wait to start reading.

When I begin a cozy mystery, I feel my shoulders relax and my attention riveted on new characters in a new location. When I finish the story it is with a sigh of satisfaction, knowing the puzzle has been solved and the guilty brought to justice.

You can find my cozy mysteries at
bonniehardywrites.com

facebook.com/bonniehardywrites

instagram.com/bonniehardywrites

goodreads.com/bonniehardy

bookbub.com/authors/bonnie-hardy

amazon.com/author/bonniehardy